Caution: Filling Is Hot

Tara Mills

Tara Mills Romance

Love stories that will captivate your heart!

http://www.taramillsromance.com

CRIMSON
ROMANCE
Avon, Massachusetts

This edition published by
Crimson Romance
an imprint of F+W Media, Inc.
10151 Carver Road, Suite 200
Blue Ash, Ohio 45242

www.crimsonromance.com

Dedication

I WANT TO THANK MY FRIENDS AND RELATIVES, READERS AND CHEERLEADERS, WHO HELPED AND ENCOURAGED ME ALONG THE WAY. A SPECIAL MENTION GOES OUT TO MY DAUGHTER-IN-LAW LYNN FOR GOING THAT EXTRA MILE AND PROOFING FOR ME TOO. AND LAST, MY BIGGEST THANK YOU TO MY HUSBAND JON, WHO WILLINGLY READS EVERYTHING I WRITE NO MATTER HOW MANY TIMES I PUT IT IN FRONT OF HIM. HONEY, IF YOU'RE GOING TO TAKE THE RIBBING FOR BEING MY INSPIRATION, HAVE FUN WITH IT AND TAKE A BOW ONCE IN A WHILE TOO.

1

There are times when you can afford to amble. Sometimes jogging is prudent. This here was a haul-ass situation. Chad Thomas checked his watch, cursed, and slammed the car door. He took off sprinting, his tie flapping in his face with the doors to Klein's Supermarket looming large ahead of him. Leaping the curb he veered away from the automatic doors, unwilling to spare even a single second waiting and pushed inside the old fashioned way. Skittering across the threshold on one foot, he executed a hard right and took off running again, shooting another impatient glance at his watch.

"Shit!"

He was seven minutes late already and rush hour traffic wasn't going to help him make up the time.

The reproduction station clock hanging right over the liquor store entrance caught his eye. He scowled at that one too. The damned thing was taunting him.

He took another hard right and danced around a customer coming out.

"Sorry, excuse me," Chad said as he raced by, already scanning the store for the nearest employee.

Bingo. Chad skidded to a breathless stop in front of the man and blurted out, "I'm in a hurry and need a hostess gift—fast."

The clerk, accustomed to demanding suburbanites, snapped his fingers, pivoted on his toe, and pointed them down the wine aisle.

He came to a stop and turned three bottles to display their labels.

"Any these will go over nicely. Price-wise they're in the same range, they're from the same region, and each is a Select of their individual vineyards. All three are popular sellers right now. You can't go wrong."

He stepped aside and Chad picked one up, turning it to read the bottle. After a moment he nodded and handed it to the clerk. "This'll be fine."

The man gave him a smug smile and took the bottle. "Good, let's get you on your way."

With his purchase in hand Chad bolted back out to the main supermarket and came to a screeching halt, his perfect pirouette the only thing that stopped his collision with a loaded shopping cart.

The sudden jolt of adrenaline left him shaken and the ambient sounds of the busy supermarket went mute, drowned out by the deafening echoes of the clog dance in his chest.

Chad pressed his hand to his heart and stared in disbelief as the shopper ambled on, still chatting on her cell phone, completely unaware of their near miss. Incredible. He shook his head. How could anyone be so oblivious? He found it more than a little frightening that she was about to get behind a steering wheel next.

The unfairness of that thought struck almost instantly. Who was he to talk? Rushing recklessly to make up lost time? He was in no position to judge.

What he needed to do was calm down, slow down, or he wasn't going to get there in one piece. That silent reminder sobered him.

Chad worked at the knot of his tie, wiggling it loose and took a deep calming breath. He was midway through his controlled exhalation when he glanced through the glass door of the store's on-site *Cook's Classroom* and his arms went slack, the wine and the time completely forgotten.

"Whoa," he whispered, entranced.

It took him a full minute to remember why he was in such a blasted hurry in the first place. When it came to him he pulled out his phone.

"Brent! It's Chad. Boy am I glad *you* answered!" Chad stepped out of the way of another cart.

"Listen, something just came up and I'm afraid I can't make dinner after all. I realize the timing sucks but could you try to smooth it over with Pam for me? ... Yeah, I know ... Hey come on—you know I wouldn't bail on you if it wasn't important ... No, I can't put it off. I'm sorry, I really am. It's something that needs my immediate attention ... Shit, did you know about this? She could have asked ... I get it but maybe I'd rather handle my own love life ... Yes but it might have been nice to know ahead of time that's all ... Tell Pam I don't need her to scare up any more dates for me okay?"

Chad groaned, angry with himself. "No—that came out wrong. Don't tell her like that. Ah, shit." He tore his eyes away from the vision behind the glass and continued. "I appreciate how much you two have worried about me but I'm okay, honestly. Let Pam know that all right? Oh, and give her a thank-you kiss from me ... Sure, thanks ... I know I know I owe you. I'll talk to you in a couple of days ... You too. Bye." He shut his phone and slipped it back into his pocket.

Every head turned when the door swung open and an impeccably dressed man walked in. Piper didn't know what unnerved her more, the way he was looking directly at her or how when their eyes met they fused, stuck firm like a wet hand on ice cold metal.

She had no idea how long she stood frozen, staring back at him before her wits returned but it didn't happen on its own. To her mortification it took the thirty-odd heads rotating back and forth between them to finally break the spell. The snickers and whispers didn't help either, leaving a sickening aftertaste of embarrassment behind.

Rattled and humiliated, Piper's eyes sparked and her flush was so intense it made her scalp tingle. Digging deep for her dignity she squared her shoulders.

"We're just getting started," she informed him, her voice

clipped and impersonal. It was the best she could manage under the circumstances. Anything more would have come out shaky. This guy was lucky she didn't hurl a chef's knife at him. "You can hang your coat on one of the hooks behind you."

She turned away deliberately, dismissing him, and smiled at an older couple seated in the front, hoping like hell they could help her refocus.

"As I was saying, my name is Piper Frost and tonight I'll be demonstrating how easy it is to use springform pans. As you know, we'll be starting with a basic cheesecake and—" she glanced around the faces and *(stupid, stupid)* faltered on that man again.

His knowing smile was both intimate and infuriating.

What an arrogant jerk! Shocked that he somehow managed to break her concentration a second time Piper wondered if it wasn't too early to despise the man. Of course, that was a silly question. She was well on her way.

Fuming, she sucked it up and continued. "Now, my cream cheese has been at room temperature—"

As it turned out, Chad was the most attentive person in the class though no doubt the worst student. Had she asked him even one relevant question such as oven temperature he couldn't have answered but he would have no trouble describing the color of Piper's eyes, the cadence of her voice, and the grace of her movements perfectly. When she looked down at her mixing bowl and applied the beaters he was lost in the incredible array of colors in her hair; the golds, browns, reds, and the purest flashes of light itself. Who knew a head of hair could be so complex?

It was obvious she was deliberately ignoring him but that didn't matter. He knew that something was happening between them. At some point she was going to forget, drop her guard, and seek him out again. When their eyes reconnected, they'd both reel from the punch. It was inevitable, indisputable. He could wait for it. He'd learned to be patient.

The oven timer went off and Piper spun to pull out a cake. Setting it on the cooling rack, she put the demonstration cake into the oven in its place and reset the timer.

Turning back to the class with a smile worthy of a professional game show hostess she picked up the edge of the pan and carefully showed the end result, pointing out the perfect color, the firm set of the filling.

"Of course we'll need to let the cake cool before we remove the rim."

Piper pulled a platter of already cut samples from the refrigerator behind her and started passing them out. Murmurs of approval broke out around the room as people chewed.

"You can find copies of this recipe as well as all the rest covered in this series in the display by the door. Feel free to take one on your way out. And of course our emergency hotline is printed on the bottom of every recipe so if you have any problems or concerns you can call and speak with one of our professionals."

Chad found it amusing that when Piper passed in front of his table with the platter she was very careful not to look at anything but his hand as he chose a sliver for himself. She swept on without meeting his eyes and Chad slid the moist sample into his mouth and grinned, pleased and encouraged that he was so obviously affecting her too.

Piper returned to the front counter. "For all of you parents here tonight, I'd like to mention the family sessions coming up. We'll be focusing on how to make fruits and vegetables appealing to kids and we encourage you to bring your children along and discover fun in the kitchen together. Often just taking part in food preparation will make a child more willing to try things they wouldn't otherwise. I highly recommend it. Thanks for coming tonight to *The Cook's Classroom*."

Piper smiled and waved off the last of her students, scattering store coupons among them like confetti until she was finally alone. She closed the door and locked herself in, expelling a sigh of relief that the arrogant jerk was out of her hair. She was dreading the end of class, assuming he was going to hover around until everyone else was gone but thankfully he left with the rest.

She turned on the faucet and filled the sink, her mind drifting backwards.

So what was his problem anyway? How could he simply waltz in here like that and totally dominate her without saying one word? She didn't like it, not at all. What really irked her was that he seemed to get off on disturbing her. Talk about psycho. It was creepy.

Once the last bowl was washed and dried Piper could finally call it a night. She shut off the lights and locked up behind her. With mere minutes left to closing, the store felt empty though there were a couple of shoppers heading for the only checkout lane still open. Piper waved goodnight to the cashier and made her way to the employee exit.

Every step she took was painful, eliciting a soft groan. She looked down at her feet, admiring her shoes but hating them too. Her suffering was so unnecessary. She knew better. Fashion meant diddly-squat when you were on your feet all day. Arch support, honey, arch support.

What a night!

Chad leaned against his fender and basked in the afterglow of his sudden and unexpected attraction. He sighed deeply, exhaling more heat into the already balmy air. If tonight was any indicator this summer was going to be a scorcher.

He wove his fingers together and stretched his arms up and over his head, bending backwards with a pleasurable moan. Then, returning to ease he rolled his sleeves up another turn, glad his tie and blazer were on his Audi's passenger seat and not on him.

Captivated by the night sky, he felt that elusive connection to the universe for the first time. The last sliver of sunlight running along the horizon held him spellbound. Then the colors deepened, flared outward before beginning a slow fade, the glow eventually and inevitably smothered by night. The sense of loss it left behind was bittersweet and so acute it staggered him.

Shaking his head philosophically, Chad took the loss in stride and refocused on the reason he lingered in this dark parking lot. He was still amazed at how the evening had shifted on him.

There was no question he needed to make it up to Brent and Pam. His culpability burned yet he found it oddly amusing that they were planning to set him up tonight and by simply stopping off for a hostess gift he ended up meeting a woman on his own anyway. Okay, maybe not exactly meeting her, that was coming, but if this went where he hoped it was headed, his friends would still get the credit for bringing them together.

Thinking back, Chad chuckled at how he'd been swept out the door with the rest of the class, only to return afterwards to find the door locked. Oh well, this was better anyway. The setting was certainly more conducive to romance. Or it was if you were moved by a starry sky. He wondered at his chances of persuading the lovely Ms. Frost to go out for a coffee or a drink with him tonight. Now that his night was free, he was open, very open, to hanging out with her for a while.

Eleven years. Could it really have been eleven years since he felt a spark like this? He thought back and saw Chelsea all over again. It was the same for them, the immediate attraction sizzling and mutual. Chad believed in love at first sight. He'd experienced it.

A heavy steel door slammed closed and he turned. The reverberations echoed across the dark sky and faded out. Chad straightened, attentive now. It was her. She walked across the parking lot, crossing out of shadow through spots of light and back into shadow again. Each brief glimpse was as tantalizing as a strip tease and sent Chad's heart rate galloping. He was amazed at how just the sight of her thrilled him.

Then his excitement transformed into sympathy as her undeniable fatigue reached out to him. Her face revealed pain with every step she took. The poor thing needed a foot massage far more than a cup of coffee that's for sure. Chad wished he could offer one but a suggestion like that would be ridiculously premature.

Piper walked gingerly across the employee lot, wincing every time her right heel landed. Muttering silently at herself and her stupidity she didn't notice the silhouette of the man loitering around the parked cars until it was too late. She paused, alert and guarded, gripping her keys so tight they bit into her fingers. She peered into the shadows, straining to identify the man before she took another step.

Of course now the insanity of wearing these shoes really hit her. Crap. There was no way she could outrun a turtle if she had to. Scanning the area, hoping to spot anyone, anyone at all in easy shouting distance in case she needed help she felt her heart sink. Double crap. Fine, she took a self-defense class once. She would know what to do if it came to that—hopefully.

Chad straightened and pushed off from his hood. Unable to bide his time a second longer he walked towards her. At least he could save her a few painful steps. She'd probably appreciate the thought, right?

The instant Piper recognized who it was her wary eyes narrowed. Of course, she should have known it would be that cocky bastard. Who else would lurk around out here? She wasn't pleased.

"Stop right there," said Piper. "I have mace and I'm not afraid to use it!"

Surprised by the threat, Chad stopped and held up his hands innocently. "Hey, sorry about that. I didn't mean to scare you. I was just waiting."

"For what?"

"For you," he said simply.

Piper glared. "Why?"

Chad's confidence wavered. "I'm beginning to wonder that myself. I was hoping we could maybe go someplace and talk."

"Talk? Forget it." She backed up. "This is *my* time and I don't mix with students socially."

He quashed his impulsive laugh. She was actually serious.

"Look, I'm not a threat but we both know we connected in there and I just wanted to invite you out so we could discuss it—that's it."

"Not interested." She turned to stalk off and he made the mistake of grabbing her arm. Her keys came up.

"Remove your hand *now* or I'll blast you," she warned ominously. Her thumb was already on the pump of the canister attached to the key ring.

He let go, taking her warning very seriously.

"I shouldn't have done that, I'm sorry, but I wasn't wrong about that connection and you know it. Everyone knew it."

She glared. "You're mistaken. Now step back."

Chad had no choice but to comply.

He didn't move until the burn of Piper's angry tail lights were long gone, absorbed into the glow of traffic.

What the hell just happened? He scratched his head and tried to figure out what he did to provoke her—anything that could account for such a violent reaction.

It might have been fear except that didn't exactly fit. She was more than capable of handling herself from what he just saw. She didn't back off like a scared rabbit but instead stood her ground and warned *him* off. That impressed him.

He knew too, absolutely knew, that their attraction was mutual. He wouldn't have waited outside for another thirty minutes for her otherwise. Of course there was the possibility that she was involved with someone else. No, Chad brushed that thought aside. A boyfriend was one of the first things she would have mentioned to discourage him and a husband, forget it. He zoomed in on her bare left hand before he even walked into her classroom tonight.

Actually, he appreciated her honesty. A lot of women would have fudged a relationship without any hesitation. Because she didn't, he just learned more about her than she probably realized.

She was an intriguing puzzle. He obviously mishandled things tonight but he could learn from it. He wasn't an idiot and more importantly, he wasn't easily run off when he wanted something— and he wanted Piper Frost. He absolutely wanted her.

Piper slapped up her turn signal and cruised through the intersection, shaking her head in bewilderment. What the hell just happened back there? Where had all that hostility come from? Her behavior was, well, let's face it, bizarre. She knew instinctively that he didn't actually pose a threat to her, at least not the physical kind. But mentally and emotionally? That was a different story altogether.

So what was really bothering her? That she found him attractive? No point denying it, she made that embarrassingly obvious to a good thirty people tonight, Mr. Beefcake included. Was it his confidence? Normally she liked a confident man but there was a difference here. It absolutely galled her to remember the knowing, proprietary look on his face, that bold assurance that she'd belong to him. Well, fat chance now, Bucko. It didn't matter in the slightest that she found him gorgeous because his attitude was a huge turnoff. Nothing chilled her down more these days than a charismatic swagger. She was smarter now and she wasn't about to fall for that song and dance again. Thanks so very much for the hard lesson, Mick!

But the ghastly truth was that the attraction was there, apparent to everyone. When she replayed the situation in her mind she saw herself as a big-screen television with all eyes trained on her until that man, whoever the hell he was, walked in holding her remote control. She could hardly fault the class for noticing whenever his thumb hit the pause/still button and she froze right in front of them. How could he manage to fluster her so badly? Wasn't that grounds enough to dislike him? If it was, why did remembering how rude she was upset her so much?

It was late when Chad got home but after looking at the clock and weighing the matter he chose to make the call anyway.

"Mom, come shopping with me tomorrow."

"Chad you really need to take out women your own age," she said in her dry mocking way.

"I'm working on it."

"Really? It's about time."

"Funny." He didn't need this from her tonight, too. "Just come with me all right?"

"Why? Give me a reason."

"Here's the thing. I kind of got off on the wrong foot with this woman I like tonight and she threatened to mace me. You're laughing, Mother?"

"Mace?"

"It's a first. So I thought if I took you shopping, you know, played the dutiful son, she might not feel so threatened by me."

There was a heavy sigh on the other end. "Fine, but you're driving."

2

Chad expected his mom to comment when he turned into Klein's Supermarket the next afternoon but Alice was strangely silent. If she was wondering why he chose to drive her all the way over here—and he'd bet money that she was—she kept it to herself. He cast an uneasy glance at her when they walked through the automatic doors but she continued to keep her thoughts to herself. He dared to hope that perhaps for once in her life she'd hold her peace.

He should have known better.

Just when he thought he was in the clear she said loud enough for all to hear, "Just look at these prices! Who can afford to shop here on a regular basis? Highway robbery, that's what this is." She frowned at Chad. "Don't shush me. I know what things cost and this is an outrage. Mark my words it's to pay for the pretty chandeliers and the fancy carpet on the floor. For crying out loud just cut the crap and maybe we can talk."

Oh, why did he think this was a good idea? What made this entire scene so utterly ridiculous is that the woman was very comfortable financially. She didn't have to worry about buying things on special or clipping coupons. She never did. His mother did those things out of principle. She would always be a frugal woman and he knew it.

Chad was practically cringing when he whispered, "Will you stop it, *please?*"

"It's your money." She threw up her hands and rolled her eyes, clearly exasperated by kids these days.

Chad picked up a basket and wandered towards the produce section.

His mom spoke up. "Since you're here you might as well pick up cream rinse for the kids."

He stopped and stared at her. "Cream rinse? What the hell is cream rinse?"

"Watch your mouth," she warned. "You know, it goes on after the shampoo."

He looked up at the elegant chandeliers adorning the ceiling and pleaded for understanding. Finally, it hit.

"Oh, you mean conditioner. It's not called cream rinse anymore."

"Whatever it's called, Missy needs a bottle. It'll keep her hair from snarling."

"You mean tangling."

"Don't annoy me—snarl works just as well as tangle. She's got long hair in case you haven't noticed. If you can't be bothered to pay attention to these things maybe you should just get it all cut off."

She dropped an artichoke into his basket.

Chad looked at it curiously, picked it up, then yelped and chucked it back again. He stared at his stinging thumb, shocked to see a drop of blood oozing out. He sucked it clean.

"Don't even go there. Missy's hair is gorgeous and what *is* that thing?" he asked, glaring at it.

"That's an artichoke and it's mine."

"You can have it. They should come with warnings. How do you even go about eating something like that without a shark suit?"

"I could show you, they're really good."

"I'll get back to you on that."

"Right."

They continued on and a bunch of asparagus joined the artichoke. "Here, one for you too," his mom said, dropping a second bunch into the basket.

Chad stopped abruptly. "It's her," he murmured to himself.

Alice turned to consider the object of her son's sudden attention. The young woman was picking through the tomatoes very carefully. Someone that finicky wasn't exactly encouraging, but hey, if she could manage to get Chad to go out once in a while that wasn't Alice's problem. Any woman able to interest her son at this point gave Alice newfound hope. It was a start anyway. About bloody time, too.

Alice sidled closer and whispered, "She's pretty." This wasn't interference. It wasn't! She was being helpful, for crying out loud. This did not constitute goading him into making a move. Oh, go to hell!

"Uh huh," Chad said absently.

The situation was veering into the Twilight Zone. It was doubtful Mr. Doesn't Miss A Thing even heard her! This was the most amusing thing she'd seen in a long time.

Alice swatted Chad on the arm to get his attention. "Romeo! Why don't you go over and talk to her before she catches you staring?"

Chad dragged his focus back to his mother and frowned. "Because she's not the most receptive woman I've ever met. I have to handle this delicately. I don't want her to think I'm stalking her so we're just going to *happen* to bump into her. Get it?"

Alice pursed her lips and contemplated her son. "*Are* you stalking her?"

His grin was the one she loved the most, the impish dimple in the corner giving him away when she would scream something as outlandish as, "Who left frogs in my bathtub?" As an only child Chad had no one to blame so he relied on his charm. It worked, damn it—every single time.

"Not yet," he said with a wink. "But I might consider it if she doesn't give me the time of day soon."

Satisfied with his answer, Alice stepped aside and waited for the show. That poor young woman didn't stand a chance.

Piper was lingering over the bell peppers when a masculine hand suddenly came around her from behind and picked up the very pepper she just set down. She pulled back and turned, all set to glare accusingly at the presumptuous shopper but her composure took a staggering hit when she saw who it was. Oh boy, he really did piss her off. She looked up at him and said imperiously, "Excuse me," and turned to stalk off.

Alice Thomas rolled her eyes and stepped forward to rescue the rapidly dissolving opportunity.

"No honey, I wanted a yellow pepper not the red." She turned her weary smile on Piper and shook her head sadly. "Men, they don't always listen do they?"

Piper eyed her suspiciously. Was this sweet little woman the arrogant prick's mother? No, no way. Then Piper looked more closely. The dimples were a match.

"Not that I've noticed," Piper mumbled and started to move along but it's not easy to shake off a determined mother.

"Wait, don't I know? You're Victoria Zimmerman right? Hazel's daughter? Yes, from Chester Park! I knew I knew you."

Hazel? Zimmerman? Who was this woman kidding? It was almost impossible to keep a straight face but Piper managed somehow—but just barely. Talk about a transparent approach. Piper never realized that mothers would willingly play wing for their sons. How disturbing was that?

"No, I'm sorry. I didn't grow up here," Piper said, still moving down the coolers.

"Oh, I'm sorry," Alice replied, right on her heels. "I swear you look just like her."

"It's okay." Piper said, biting her lip but smiling just the same. "No sweat." Then she was gone, escaping through the Employees Only doors.

Chad watched her leave, not necessarily discouraged but stumped about what tactic to try next.

Alice looked at her son and shrugged.

At least his stop at the store wasn't a complete waste of time.

Chad dropped by the deli and bought a sandwich for his lunch before driving his mom home. He wolfed it down on his way to the site, arriving just in time for his meeting with the architect.

Twenty minutes later they were bent over Chad's hood looking at the plans spread out across the top when he heard someone shouting his name. Chad looked up and saw the stocky man dressed in stiff denims, a sweat-stained shirt, and a hardhat rushing over.

"What is it, Bill?" Chad asked.

Bill gulped for air. His words came out in a breathless rush. "Hanson wants you right away in the southeast corner."

Chad slid the plans back to the architect. "That looks good. I'll let Dwyer know about the plumbing changes. Excuse me."

He slipped on his hardhat and followed Bill across the work site, skirting an excavator on its way down an earthen ramp and into what would eventually be underground parking. A line of dump trucks were waiting to follow it down, ready to be filled.

When they reached the southeast crater Bill pointed into it just as Hanson looked up and saw them. He waved Chad down. Chad took a second to pick the easiest route into the hole before hitting the slope. Still, there was no way to stop the dirt from leaking into his shoes on the way to the bottom.

"What've you got?" Chad asked.

"You're not gonna like this," Hanson warned. "Foundation's still here from the brewery that burned down in the teens."

"We knew that."

Hanson nodded. "But we didn't expect them to have filled it in with whatever the hell they wanted to throw away. We're coming across old railroad ties and spikes, assorted steel machinery all twisted and tangled, cables and—" He set off at a brisk walk with Chad hurrying after him. Then Hanson stopped and pointed at the rusty edges of several old barrels partially exposed in the crude dirt wall in a haphazard way.

"They're not empty," Bill said ominously.

A sudden chill swept through Chad as he stared in alarm at what they'd dug up. "What the hell is that?"

"No fucking clue but obviously we can't proceed now, at least not until we get the go-ahead from the state. Minimum—this puts us off schedule by two weeks just for excavation, if we're lucky. My guess is closer to six weeks, especially if there were leaks."

Chad swore. "McPherson's not gonna like this."

"That's why I like my job just fine, boss." Hanson was grinning, suddenly glad that he wasn't the one who had to deliver the bad news to "The Money."

Chad groaned. "All right, I've got some calls to make. In the meantime, why don't you concentrate on the northeast? That section wasn't part of the same property so it should be clean."

"I already sent the three-sixty over there to join the other excavator."

Chad shook his head. "I forgot. I saw it on my way over." He rubbed his brow with a heavy hand then took a deep breath. "Let me know right away if you find any more nasty surprises."

"Will do."

Chad let loose with a muttered string of curses as he climbed back up to grade. It pissed him off that they were hitting a snag so early in the project.

The phone in his pocket started vibrating. He pulled it out and cupped his ear so he could hear over the noise.

"Chad Thomas."

"Daddy?"

"Missy?"

"Yeah."

"Why are you calling? You know you're not allowed to use your phone in school."

"I need my Dora sleeping bag. Can you bring it to Grandma's?"

Chad looked around and returned the nod of a crewman.

"This couldn't wait?"

"I need it," she whined.

"Fine, I'll drop it off. Now hang up like a good girl before you get us both into trouble."

She giggled. "I'm calling from the bathroom."

"Good-bye, Missy," he said firmly.

Deep lines cut in around Chad's reluctant smile as he shut his phone. He couldn't decide which of his eight-year-olds was going to challenge him more. Right now, Kenny was a typical boy. But Chad had a hunch it would be Missy that worried the hell out of him once she hit her teens.

Piper loved visiting Highland Park on her rare nights off. Soon, soon she was going to have a lot more of those.

Now, after seven, the evening sunlight fell across the choppy water, making it glitter and shine. It was stunning. Rejuvenated by everything around her, Piper beamed up into the broad oak, elm, and maple leaves twisting and fluttering in that same breeze. She gloried in it, relishing the way it ruffled her hair. In some deep, profound way she knew she was home. Funny, because this was a new city for her, miles away from her home base, her family, her old life. Yet, there it was again, that deep sense that she was right where she was meant to be.

Piper ambled along the serpentine path past the sandy beach. She smiled at the group of young girls packing it up for the night, shaking the sand out of their towels while an iPod played music from a colorful bag on the ground.

The smell of Coppertone carried her away to another beach, another group of young girls racing over the hot sand in their bare feet. Memories of how good the cool water felt were so vivid Piper stretched her toes in her shoes as if standing in it now. The music might have changed, and that wasn't Gretchen's boom box slowly cooking away, but the rest? No.

It seemed only yesterday that she and her friends went shopping by themselves. She laughed now at how seriously they took finding that one perfect suit, but they all wanted to look more grown up and though they didn't say it aloud—sexy. Piper remembered how her triumph turned to bitter disappointment once her parents had their say. Her impassioned pleas ineffective, she shuffled back to the store with her mother to exchange her beloved bikini for a more modest one-piece.

Now, as an adult, she understood her parents' objections. They were worried, that's all. Of course the girls wanted to accentuate their budding assets and catch the eyes of the boys but at the time it seemed that their parents were clearly against them. They didn't understand! Piper smiled to herself. Of course they did. The girls wanted to be liked, pursued, and maybe even kissed. Their parents, however, wanted nothing of the kind. Too bad they didn't have a lot of say in the matter. Even though the girls couldn't pray their way into an A cup they still managed to gain admirers. Piper nurtured warm thoughts of that lost summer of early adolescence and those innocent breathy sighs of her youth. Why do we all have to grow out of that?

She turned and watched a young father run past, his hand on the back of the bicycle seat, struggling to keep up with his son as the child pedaled furiously away while teetering on his training wheels. That's how it is. Life goes on and pretty soon that little boy will forget all about his bike helmet and reach timidly for some girl's hand for the first time too.

An old-fashioned carriage, ornate with its bright red and gold detailing was selling fresh popcorn near the curb. It looked to be a popular stop for moms with strollers but just as Piper was being lured over by the intoxicating aroma she heard the crack of a bat followed by the answer of a crowd coming from behind the grove of trees on her left. Interested, she turned her feet that way instead and followed the winding path.

Why not? Community baseball at its finest. To her surprise there was a pretty good crowd in the bleachers. Piper took a second to study the stands then headed up to the top of the risers so she could have a backrest. The sun was low enough now that it hit her right in the face. She regretted not wearing sunglasses. Using her hand as a visor Piper read the scoreboard. The Bobcats were ahead by one run at the top of the seventh.

Piper's mouth dropped open when she saw the man from class rise from his team bench and take the field. He tossed an ice pack onto the grass against the fence and limped over to third, slipping his hand into his glove. The very sight of him gave her a chill that raised both goose bumps and her nipples simultaneously.

Was there no mercy in the world? Now, completely annoyed, all she wanted to do was slip off without him seeing her but it was probably too late for that. She decided to wait it out and see what happened. Moving might just make her more conspicuous. The last thing she wanted to do was deal with this guy again.

3

"Chad!"

A call from the mound dragged Chad's attention back from the stands just in time to snatch the ball out of the air and whip it across to first. He spared a second look at the crowd and confirmed the impossible. That was definitely Piper—no doubt about it—and she looked terrific with her hair down.

His knee hurt like a son of a bitch but he smiled anyway, very aware of this golden opportunity to impress the hell out of her. This was his game, this was his base, and he was good. Now he'd be great because nothing motivated a guy more than the chance to show off for a woman.

The first batter walked out to the plate and went into his stance. Chad spread his legs, knees bent, ready to move in any direction. He was tense, every muscle in his body poised to react. Only when the batter struck out did Chad hazard another look at Piper.

The next man up hit a single over second base. Finally, Chad's moment to shine came when the third batter blasted the ball right at him. Chad leaped into the air, caught it, then twisted and in one fluid motion rifled it to second before he even landed on his feet. The runner was tagged stretching for the base—a gorgeous double play.

Feeling inordinately pleased, Chad trotted off the field, accepting the congratulatory back slaps from his teammates as his due. The smile he bestowed on everyone was bright enough to strain the power grid.

Ugh, Piper thought with distaste. So, he was the arrogant jock type. She should have figured. One of those guys with the "use 'em and lose 'em" mentality. Still, it made perfect sense considering the mantle of entitlement he wore draped across his shoulders. Piper slipped away as the other team took the field.

When Chad's turn at bat came he walked out confidently but his swagger turned into a sorrowful plod when he tried, and failed, to spot her. It was no good, he knew she was gone. He deflated like a balloon, his adrenaline rush a distant memory.

Piper was in a deep sleep when four minutes shy of one a.m. she let out an earthy moan that startled her awake. She rolled inside the sheets, her body sticky with perspiration despite her nudity.

Damn him! It was extremely rare for Piper to have provocative dreams but several in a row? Unheard of! If that wasn't disturbing enough all she had to do was recall the last in that alarming series and cringe. That horrifying spectacle actually strayed into the pornographic. Was it any wonder, judging by the images still burned on her brain, that her heart was racing the 10K? No matter how hard she tried to exorcize the image of his strong thighs, calves, and even worse, his bare flexing buttocks from her brain it didn't work. He was haunting her, taunting her.

Piper expelled a deep frustrated breath and kicked back the covers. This was not good. Dreaming of him? What was that all about? She didn't want this and she certainly didn't want him. Did she? No way. But her pulse told her otherwise. She definitely had in her dreams. Just remembering the way she writhed against him like a cat in heat disgusted her. It didn't matter that it never happened if she herself planted the idea, the images in her own mind.

She needed air. Stomping to the window she snapped on the air conditioner and leaned into the blast. The hum soothed her while the cool stream lifted her damp hair from her face and shoulders. She pulled her hair up and let her neck take a direct blast. Yes, yes, *this* was moan-worthy—not what she was dreaming of doing with what's his name! Oh baby, this was good.

Only when she was completely cooled off did she go back to bed but before she settled down she gave her pillow a sharp look and a solid punch for good measure, putting it on notice that she'd brook no more of that nonsense. Finally satisfied, Piper dropped her head into the pocket she created and closed her eyes.

Unless one of the kids was sick nothing woke Chad during the night so when he jerked awake from a sound sleep feeling restless and tense he wandered down the dark hallway to look in on his children. It wasn't until he saw the empty bunk beds in Kenny's room that he remembered they were spending the night with their grandma.

He scratched his mussed up head and frowned. Something set his heart rate spiking. He wondered if he should phone his mom to see if everything was okay. No—better not. She would have called him. Waking her up at this time of night would only panic her and she wasn't a young woman anymore.

Rubbing his hand over his face he headed into the hall bathroom, stepped around the bath toys on the mat and filled a SpongeBob Dixie cup with cold water. He downed it in one go without shutting off the stream. After two more gulps from the faucet he finally turned off the tap and shuffled back to his room. He scratched his chest absently, suddenly confronted by another mystery.

Normally a sound sleeper, Chad didn't move much during the night but for some reason his bedding was a mess. It looked like he'd been in some kind of wrestling match. Perplexed, he bent down to re-tuck the sheets and sort out the blankets when out of nowhere a bewildering chuckle burbled out of him. He froze in surprise.

"What the hell?"

Now this was getting weird.

4

Chad breathed a deep contented sigh and slipped out of his blazer, tossing it through the window and onto the back seat. An easy smile warmed his handsome face as he flicked open a third button on his shirt then moved on to his cuffs. He rolled back his sleeves because he needed to feel this air, this sunshine on his bare skin. What a fantastic day.

It was a gift really, utterly beautiful and not even two o'clock in the afternoon. With a little hustle he was able to clear up his work earlier than expected which left an hour and a half of free time before the kids got home from school. His plan was simple, certainly, but sometimes that was all one needed to recalibrate the machinery. Chad was more than ready to exchange the noise and dust of the construction site with a breezy drive around Scenic Lake. It wasn't that much farther off his route but sometimes the heart aches for those tranquil moments and he was listening to his for a change.

He let his arm drape out his open window as he drove, toasting it brown in the sunshine. He dipped and dunked his hand into the wind, playing the stream of resistance like a dolphin breaking waves. Chad felt alive to sensations, keenly aware of the cooler temperature close to the shore and attuned to the hair on his forearm rippling and waving like a field of tall grass.

It was interesting but right somehow that the depth of the blues of the water and the sky should clutch at his chest, engage him emotionally. He was captivated, his eyes straying repeatedly to the lake, until something else grabbed his attention—Piper's car parked along the curb.

He knew it was hers right away by the faded hat in the back window but the license plate clinched it. He got a good long look at it the other night when she sped off. The creases around his smile deepened when he saw an open space two cars ahead of hers. Chad threw on his blinker.

With so many people out enjoying the perfect weather, the chances that he'd find Piper were slim. She could be halfway around the lake by now. Still, Chad tipped up his sunglasses and got out, scanning the faces for the only one that mattered. He wandered across the grass, lifting his chin to the sun for one glorious moment before making his way to the nearest bench. He sat down and stretched out his legs, leaning against the back and soaking up the atmosphere. Chad shifted his gaze to a couple of windsurfers moving away from shore.

His jaw dropped. There she was, cutting through the water with her feet spread comfortably on her board, leading her friend out. She was wearing a skin hugging wet suit with long sleeves but cut high at the legs. Chad sat up and squinted, trying to get a better look but the life vest interfered so he moved on, grinning at her wet ponytail and utterly dazzled by the quick flashes of her radiant smile.

He leaned back again and spread his arms out across the back of the bench, making himself comfortable. When Piper whooped and laughed so did he, vicariously enjoying her happiness. Only when Piper and her friend were specks on the other side of the lake did Chad finally check the time. He swore and jumped up, racing for his car.

Piper was giddy—pure and simple. Surfing was the closest she could come these days to the exhilaration she loved chasing as a kid. Once she flew recklessly down long, steep hills on her bicycle without ever touching the brakes. The speed, the risk of a car pulling out in front of her had always been at the back of her mind but it fed something wild in her. Age and a sense of her mortality eventually tempered her childish taste for thrills, or so she thought, until she discovered windsurfing. The charge wasn't always there but when it reared up powerfully and she wrestled with it, there was nothing better.

She had to give Mick grudging credit for introducing her to the sport. It was big kid fun and one of the few highs in their otherwise rollercoaster relationship. Still, even for a person who got off on the plunging stomach sensation, living that way was unendurable on a daily basis. It was depressing to think that had he not screwed up the last time, royally, she'd still be making excuses for him and feeling guilty about wanting to quit his merry-go-round.

When had he stopped being her partner and become her responsibility? If he hadn't given her the nudge she needed to break free she'd still be supporting the prick. Okay, maybe she should thank him for his philandering too.

But the truth was that Mick was at his best on those rare occasions when he took over. He taught her with the patience of a saint how to get up on her board, how to feel and enjoy the power of nature as she worked with it to invite motion. They laughed when she tumbled off repeatedly and he was supportive and encouraging when she tried again. So what if she wasn't a natural. She knew what she was doing now and it pleased her. She'd grown strong and the muscles in her legs and thighs were more defined and she was proud of her sculpted arms. She liked the tone that came with the exercise. Even more, she liked the freedom. She never felt so unencumbered in her life, so liberated.

She glanced over at her friend and gave the signal to head back. Joy nodded and Piper turned. As the sail caught the wind with a snap Piper was struck by the mood to race. She let out a giddy yell as she took off, leaving Joy in her metaphorical dust.

Chad hung up the phone and sighed, kicking back in his chair and pinching the bridge of his nose. It wasn't easy, but he'd dealt with McPherson.

"Daddy." Missy came storming through the door in a huff.

He sat up. "What are you doing in here? You know I'm working."

"Kenny's pointing at me."

His chair creaked as he leaned forward and laid his cheek on his hand. "And?"

"He's pointing at me!" she explained again as if he were dimwitted.

"In what way?"

She demonstrated, her fingers making a gun.

"Kenny!" Chad bellowed then looked at his daughter shrewdly. "You enjoy getting your brother into trouble, don't you?"

"Sometimes." A flash of a smile stole across her face before she hid it away.

His son, Missy's twin, popped into the office.

"I didn't do anything." His automatic response to everything.

"Were you shooting your finger at your sister?" God, that sounded ridiculous out loud.

"I don't know."

Chad felt drained. "Just don't do it again, okay?"

"Okay."

"Okay, Missy?" He looked at his daughter.

"Okay."

Kenny was just turning when Chad caught the sneer he gave his sister.

"That's enough! You two have to start getting along better because I'm sick of being a referee."

"What's a referee?" Missy asked.

"A zebra," Kenny answered and they walked out, pals again as he explained exactly what the men in striped shirts did.

Chad shut down his computer and desk lamp. He followed them out and closed the door to his office behind him.

While he made dinner, Missy hung over the counter watching.

"You make the best sandwiches." She grinned and slithered over the counter on her belly. He could see her feet coming up behind her like two purple antennas.

"Do I?" he asked absently. "Sit on that stool the right way please."

She slid back onto her butt. "Yeah, you butter every spot of bread so there aren't any dry places and you do my sandwich first."

"I learned."

He couldn't stop the wry smile when it popped up as he recalled the day he made her sandwich second and with the same knife he used for Kenny's. His son wasn't nearly as picky. Missy was firmly against mayonnaise.

Now it was time, the crucial moment of truth. He looked at her and asked, "How do you want it cut today?"

She tilted her head to the side and thought about it, carefully. "Small triangles."

After he cut it to her specifications he slid the plate towards her and she picked up a soft section. "Mmm good."

"Kenny," he called.

The boy ran like a herd of buffalo through the house. How could one eight-year-old boy make such a racket?

The kid came sliding into the kitchen on his stocking feet. He didn't stop until the edge of his foot hit the bottom of the cabinets.

"Yes!" Kenny punched the air excitedly. "Did you see how far I went?"

"Impressive," Chad said. "How do you want your sandwich cut?"

"In half." He climbed up onto his stool and dug into the bag of Fritos.

"In half how?" Chad asked. He showed all the ways it could be cut.

Kenny looked at his sister's sandwich and chose straight down the middle instead of diagonally, just to be different. Chad didn't understand why everything had to be the opposite with them but for some reason it did.

He ate his own sandwich—uncut—while leaning against the counter and staring out the window into the backyard.

"Can I be excused?" Kenny asked with his mouth full.

Without turning Chad said, "Don't talk until you've swallowed. You know that. And you have to finish your milk first. All of it."

Kenny chugged his milk noisily. "Done."

Chad gave him a distracted nod and Kenny dropped down to the floor and took off.

"That was very good. Thank you, Daddy," Missy complimented in the kiss-ass style she'd adopted recently.

He thanked her without getting into it.

A minute later Chad turned to clear the dishes and was surprised that she was still sitting on her stool, watching him thoughtfully.

"What is it, kiddo?"

"I was just wondering why pretty women don't chase you."

Chad sputtered. "What?"

"Why don't pretty women chase you and want to kiss you?"

"Honey, if I knew that, I'd tell you."

She looked him over carefully. "Maybe you're just too old but I don't think so."

He smiled, charmed. "You don't think I'm old?"

"No, you're old." She shook her head, completely erasing his smile. "But so are a lot of pretty ladies. Someone should like you."

"Why are you asking about this?"

"I got to watch *Sex and the City* at Cassidy's."

"Her mother let you watch *Sex and the City*?"

"No, her mom was watching it and she sent us to play quiet in Cassidy's room. We turned it on up there just to see what it was about."

Missy opened the sugar dish and licked her finger then dipped the moistened tip into the very center. She poked the granule-coated finger into her mouth. Chad stared at her, momentarily stunned, then took the cover and clapped it back on top and pulled the sugar dish away from her.

"Don't ever let me see you do that again."

"Do you miss kissing Daddy?"

Did nothing faze her?

Chad scratched behind his ear and wondered how to answer that question. He finally opted for the truth. "Yeah, I guess I do."

She flashed her still perfect little smile at him, her dimples sinking deep.

Sleepovers were going to be changing after this. Maybe he was a little too reluctant to host them here and a little too enthusiastic when Missy wanted to spend the night elsewhere. What else had he screwed up?

"Dad, what's lingerie?"

Chad scrambled for the right answer. "Underwear," he said finally.

"Oh." She slipped off of her stool, clearly disappointed. "I thought it might be something special."

"Nope. Just plain, old-fashioned underwear."

"Boring."

"Yeah."

She left him to clean the kitchen and sweat over everything that seemed to be snowballing all at once. He needed to spend more quality time with his kids, feed them more than sandwiches for every meal just because they liked it and he didn't feel like battling over the menu.

Slowly, a smile crept across his face. Of course, it was so simple, so obvious. Things were about to change, for all of them if he had a say in the matter.

5

Relaxing under the pavilion at the park with the lake as a backdrop Joy finished the last bite of fruit salad and pressed the lid down on the empty plastic container. She released a contented sigh. "That was really good."

Piper smiled. "Thanks. Just wait, summer's just around the corner and we're going to have a lot more fresh fruits available."

"I love this time of year."

"Berries."

"Mmm, berries," Joy agreed.

Still blissed out from their afternoon on the lake Piper tipped her head back, closed her eyes, and squirted a stream of bottled water directly into her mouth. "You know what sucks about living in an apartment?"

"Hmm?"

"No pantry," said Piper.

"I'm in a townhouse and I don't have a pantry either."

"Short sighted."

"No kidding."

They mulled over their loss silently for a moment before Joy spoke up.

"I'd love a root cellar."

"A root cellar? I could see that. Do you can?"

"No, but my grandma did. Of course she had a garden. She had fresh herbs, vegetables, and fruits most of the year and what she couldn't serve fresh came out later in a jar."

"Good?"

"Awesome."

"My mom was the queen of the can opener. What she didn't

microwave she boiled."

"So where'd you come from?"

"My friends' moms. I practically begged them to invite me to spend the night—I was shameless—just so I could eat real home cooking. Gretchen's mom was my favorite. She was so down to earth, a real hippie type. She let me hang around in her kitchen and bombard her with questions. I really appreciated that she never made me feel stupid but I guess it was common knowledge by then that my mom wasn't exactly the domestic type. Anyway, I showed an interest and she sort of nurtured me. Mrs. Copeland was the first person I told when I decided to enroll in culinary school."

"And that's where you met Mick."

"And we were having such a nice time here."

"He's part of that past."

"He is," Piper acknowledged grudgingly.

They both fell into silence. After a couple of minutes Joy suddenly slapped the picnic table, making Piper jump.

"Hey, before I forget I wanted to ask, how about doubling this weekend? A friend of Dom's is coming to town. Might be fun."

Piper grimaced. "Not interested."

Joy rolled her eyes. "Come on. Your bout of celibacy has to be growing old by now."

Piper laughed. "Sure, but it's not stale enough to tempt me into a blind date."

"Consider it a chance to get out and do something—enjoy some fresh company for a change."

"Fresh? Did I just hear you right? What is he, the man with a million hands?"

Joy laughed. "Cut it out. I meant that he's a really nice guy. Who knows, you might just hit it off."

Piper sighed. "I'm sure he's great but I just don't care right now. I'm enjoying my independence, my freedom."

"That's why he'd be perfect for you. He lives six hours away so you only have to get together occasionally, if you know what I mean."

Piper shuddered. "What a revolting idea. Nope, I'm simply not interested in a man for any reason right now but I'll let you know if and when that changes, okay?"

When Joy eyed her skeptically Piper went on. "Hear me out. My apartment is clean—all the time. I only have to do laundry for one. I love, absolutely love that the toilet isn't foul—ever. I can cook whatever I like without having to consult with anyone else. Plus, I have the entire bed to myself and I'm using every glorious inch of it!"

"That doesn't depress you?"

"No way. For the first time in two years I have a savings account that's growing, not shrinking. It's great to finally get ahead financially. I don't want another relationship where I'm the only grownup, making sure the bills are paid on time and floating him until payday. It's not nice grinding your teeth down to nothing when you have to explain for the millionth time where the toilet paper is and how to replace it."

"I'm not asking you to move in with the guy and buy towels together. Besides, not every guy is Mick."

"I know that but people have a way of falling into patterns and I don't plan on being one of them. Mick exhausted me. I'm drained, and I have nothing else to give right now. I need some selfish time to recover. I simply can't worry about anyone else for a while. That's all."

"That's screwed up."

"Come on. Try to understand. Mick was a mistake—granted. I suppose we all need one to shake us up, screw with our perceptions a little, but in the end, those bad boys make lousy partners. I did learn something important from him, though. If a guy can make your blood sizzle with a single smile, you'd better run, *fast*, in the opposite direction. No way are you going to make rational decisions when your hormones are popping like firecrackers. I'm not letting Mick launch me into a bad habit. Nope. When I'm finally ready to commit to someone else, I'll be smart about it. No more hormonal surges and brain-numbing lust for me."

"So you guard yourself against all possibilities when they arise. That doesn't sound smart, that sounds *scared*. You sound like you don't trust yourself to recognize distinctions."

"You think it's easy to gauge? Tell me, how soon can I ask a guy whether he willingly does his own laundry, cooks, cleans up after himself, or would contribute to the household finances if we got together—first date? I'd like to consider that the elimination round but one word on what really matters will send any sane guy screaming for the hills."

She took another squirt. "How about this, can he hold down a steady job? Mick couldn't do that and he's ten times the chef I am. I hated—I can't stress hated enough here so I'll say it again—*hated* that he's so talented and at the same time unwilling to use those talents if it even threatened to interfere with his play. I can't afford another man in my life like that."

"So tell me what you're looking for."

Piper frowned, her mind racing to describe the impossible dream just to throw Joy off her case. "First of all, I remind you that I'm not looking. Agreed?"

"Agreed."

"But, if I had to describe my perfect man I'd say that he's gainfully employed, considerate, and mature." She waved her finger at her friend. "But here's where it gets tricky. He has to be stable and interesting at the same time. I'd like him to be informed and exciting, naughty and nice, *faithful*. He'd respect my opinions even when we disagree and respect me as his equal partner and not a subordinate in my own home. I won't be my mother. She couldn't answer a simple question without conferring with my dad or passing the decision-making off to him entirely. It really used to piss me off."

"You're kidding right?"

Piper took a deep breath and shook her head sadly. "I wish. I never understood it. She liked the master of the house bit. When I was a teenager I used to try pushing her to be her own person but it never helped. All it did was strain our relationship and we didn't come to terms with who we both are until after I moved out on my own."

"Well, keep me posted anyway." Joy gave her a sympathetic smile. "I'm sure I can rake someone up for you if you're willing."

"When I'm ready, I'll let you know."

Piper capped her water, confident that this ideal man didn't exist and if he did, and that was a seriously gargantuan *if*, she wasn't ready for him yet.

6

Can anything else possibly go wrong tonight?

Piper raced through the store with yet another jar of applesauce tucked under her arm.

"Hi, yes, nice to see you," she said, acknowledging a frequent class attendee coming down the canned goods aisle.

Piper breezed by and checked her watch. Time to hustle.

"Stupid slippery glass jar," she muttered, visualizing its slow motion roll then the horrifying *aaah* moment just before it went plunging over the edge of the counter and shattered on the floor. She had to admit, the spray of pulverized apple exceeded even her expectations. It hit everything, the bottoms of chairs, the cabinets, and a good eight feet of floor not to mention the front of her legs and shoes. The impressive starburst pattern was really quite pretty actually but of course even the hurried mop up she did put her way behind schedule. She would have to do it properly after class. In the meantime she didn't relish finding sticky spots with her shoes all night.

Naturally, considering the way the evening started, it figured she'd be the last to arrive on the first night of their kid-friendly series. Being late in general irked her but knowing she had families coming in tonight, well, that really bothered her. Piper pushed through the door with a smile pasted on her face and walked straight up the middle of the room to the front counter. She could feel the eyes of the entire class following her.

One sticky spot identified. Damn it!

She set the applesauce down and turned her smile up another degree.

"Look at all the young faces. This is great! I'm sorry I wasn't here to greet you personally but I had a little accident." She patted

the top of the jar. "But no harm done and I can't wait to get started. Show of hands, how many of you have cooked before?"

Piper laughed at all the hands suddenly in the air. "Sorry, I was talking to the kids. Moms and dads you can sit this one out." All the hands went down but the laughter raised the volume in the room considerably. "Let's try again, okay? Any kids here tonight with cooking experience?"

Only a few little hands went up this time.

Piper smiled. "That's awesome. You're going to feel right at home but if you're new to cooking, no worries, you're in for a real treat. Tonight we're going to make muffins and you're going to see just how easy cooking can be. But here's the most important rule, you should never cook without an adult around, okay?"

Catching movement out of the corner of her eye, Piper turned and saw that Mr. Persistent was back and shifting on his stool to see around the woman in front of him. And that was it. Their eyes locked and every thought in her head fled on a coffee break without a backwards shrug. Wonderful.

Then he abruptly broke the connection, releasing Piper because, because there was a small girl tugging on his sleeve? No way. Yes, apparently way. The girl cupped her mouth and whispered in his ear. He nodded back and was right in the middle of his reply when they both vanished, blocked out by the woman in front of them and her spectacular perm.

Piper gave herself a mental head slap. How did she manage to miss Mr. Marvelous on her way in? Wait a second, hold it. What was she doing? Duh! Class, teaching, *focus*.

The delay cost her. Half a heartbeat later he leaned back into the aisle, located Piper, and reclaimed her attention. Caught like a fish on his hook, she tried to fight herself free without success. Not until he gave her a slow intimate smile did she manage it, the annoyance that smile provoked finally snapping his line.

Wrenching her eyes away, Piper skidded over the other

heretofore unnoticed child at that table. Appalled by her lousy powers of observation her face warmed another five degrees. She was out of control. Seriously out of control here. It was intolerable. She wasn't going to put up with this.

So what if he brought a pint-sized entourage? That didn't change the fact that she had a job to do. Still, she couldn't tamp down her resentment. The jerk was toast, burnt toast! She should have known things would crap out tonight as soon as she broke that jar of applesauce. Talk about your bad omens.

She needed to get a grip, take back the reins and run the guy down. Mmm, not a bad fantasy actually. She wasn't going to lose this power struggle. No way. Piper regulated her breathing and took a second to stretch her arms towards the floor, tightening her muscles and extending her fingers until even the skin burned. Only then did she trust herself to speak.

With a stiff smile for her staring class Piper returned to the job at hand. "Normally I'd simply demonstrate for you but tonight we're going to do something different. You'll be working in teams and everyone will have a chance to participate. Now I'd like someone from each station to come up and get the supplies you'll need."

A murmur of voices filled the room and then each group dispatched someone to the counter to collect their boxes of ingredients.

She tried to ignore her personal pest when he stood to come forward but a nasty impulse took over when he got up there and she and couldn't help sneering, "What'd you do now, rent a couple of kids for the night?"

He turned with an amused smirk. "No, they're mine."

Piper's eyebrows scrambled up her forehead. Why did that news throw her? She stared after him as he walked back to his children. Then she did yet another unthinkable thing. She checked out his ass. Great idea, why not just add an erratic heart rate to go with everything else tonight? The last thing she wanted was some castoff whose wife finally told him, "Thanks but no thanks," when she came to her senses.

It was so much easier, far more comfortable, for Piper to nurture the suspicion that he hauled his kids here just to score points with her. He was using them to humanize himself. Well, fat chance! All it did was make her loathe him even more. She refused to consider for a second that his was just one of the many parent/child combinations filling her classroom tonight. As far as Piper was concerned, the man had no scruples. The scumbag was going down!

But, she reminded herself, she was a professional. She was above it. She'd take the high road and let him try to make peace with his polluted conscience. Piper cleared him from her mind and moved on.

"In case you're wondering," she said with a bright smile, "this is a liquid measuring cup and these here are for dry measuring. Do not confuse the two."

Undaunted by the half-hearted chuckles she pressed on. "Now, with muffins, it's very important not to over-mix your batter. You'll have some lumps but don't worry, that's perfectly normal."

She ladled the batter into the paper cups and looked out at the attentive faces.

"Now I need someone to help me set the timer. Anyone?"

She pointed to a young girl before her furious hand waving caused an injury. "How about you?"

The girl joined her at the front counter.

"Have you ever set an oven timer before?" Piper asked her.

The girl shook her head, suddenly shy.

"It's easy. Here, we'll show everyone together. First, look at the recipe. How long does it say we need to bake these?" To help the child out Piper underscored the type with her fingernail.

The little girl hooked her hair behind her ear and leaned forward to see. "Eighteen to twenty minutes," she read carefully.

"Perfect!" Piper said and slid her tray into the smaller of the ovens and closed the door.

They set the timer together and the girl skipped back to her parents with an excited smile.

One after another, each group sent their muffins forward, little toothpick flags distinguishing them from the rest, and they were placed into the other two ovens. While they baked, Piper passed around a platter of already prepared banana chocolate chip muffins for everyone to sample.

"There's a sheet of muffin recipes which includes the applesauce ones we just made and I encourage you to take a copy home with you."

The timer went off and Piper pulled all the tins from the oven. "As these cool, you can come up and collect your own."

One by one, adults came forward to drop off their supply boxes and pick up their muffins while Piper continued to discuss using other fruits in recipes, from bananas to apples, raisins, even craisins.

"Don't get locked into blueberries alone," she warned. "Muffins are a healthy alternative to cookies and we have more control over fat and sugar when we make snacks ourselves."

Mr. Mom came for his plate of muffins and carried them back to his table.

Piper hated how often her eyes strayed his way but she couldn't seem to stop it, especially now that her frosty attitude was suffering some serious cracks just seeing the warm interplay going on in their corner. She hardened her heart but it wasn't even five minutes later that a major fault line opened up when his spontaneous laughter tore her attention away from the woman speaking to her and Piper turned just in time to see the little girl stuffing a muffin into his mouth. The kid was feeding him for god's sake!

They were close, no doubt about that. Even when he was directing their cleanup the kids were eager to do what he asked. Her eyes followed him again when he got up to take their napkins to the garbage can.

Five minutes later Piper dismissed the class and stood by the door slipping recipes into open hands and chatting briefly with those inclined to chat. Then she turned and her heart dropped into her stomach. Damn, that guy was hanging back with his kids, waiting for everyone else to leave. This did not bode well.

The little girl skipped and jumped around him. "Can we do this again Daddy?"

"We'll see."

Caught watching them, Piper looked away self-consciously. Studying her for a moment he sent the kids out with a quick word then walked over and faced her.

To call what she felt discomfort would be a gross understatement. Piper felt ashamed and embarrassed by her lack of self-control. She'd acted like a complete witch from the very beginning and tonight was merely a delightful continuation on that theme. There could only be one reason he wanted to send his kids out of hearing. She steeled herself for the verbal abuse she knew she deserved.

"Do you have a class tomorrow?"

His question surprised her.

Piper looked up in confusion. "No."

He cocked an eyebrow at her and smiled. "Then can we take you out?"

"*What?*" Okay, that sounded a little rude but this was the last thing she expected.

"We'd like to take you out," he said, pantomiming to help the slow-witted.

Piper fought hard not to smile and failed. "I'm sorry, *we?*"

"Afraid so. We're kind of a unit but guess what, you'll be perfectly safe with two undersized chaperones. What do you say?"

"Who *are* you?" It was probably time she asked.

He laughed and offered his hand. "Chad Thomas. It's nice to finally meet you."

Still holding her hand he stretched his head out the doorway and called, "Hey, you two, get in here a second."

They must have been just outside because they were quick. They looked at her with interest.

Chad released her hand and explained to his munchkins, "I

just asked Ms. Frost to hang out with us tomorrow night. What do you think?"

The girl sized Piper up and down slowly. "Do you watch *Sex and the City*?"

Chad's eyes bulged and he clamped a hand over the child's mouth.

Piper laughed. "I'm afraid not. I usually work nights."

The boy shook his head at his sister. "I'm Kenny."

"Hi, Kenny." Piper smiled at him.

He pointed his thumb at his sister apologetically. "That's Missy."

"Hello, Missy."

Chad's eyes were twinkling when he carefully removed his hand from his daughter's mouth. "So, what do you say?"

Piper didn't know who he was addressing since he'd asked everyone a question but when she accepted she was drowned out by the two kids who also answered with a resounding, "Yes!"

Chad had Piper write down her telephone number on the back of their recipe sheet. Ushering his kids out the door, he called back to her, "Dress casual, very casual."

Surely this wasn't a date. Did he think this was a date? Don't be stupid, Piper, what man would ask a woman out when he had his kids tagging along? Forget it. She was getting paranoid, that's all. But if, and this was really a big if, he was thinking along those lines she could just nip it in the bud. Hanging out with them did not put her under any obligations. For crying out loud, he made sure she understood that she'd be safe in their company. She had to stop being so suspicious. It didn't look good on her. Why was she trying so hard to define a simple invitation anyway? The chance to meet new people came at the right time and now she actually had plans for a change. How cool was that? A win-win situation, really. One question though: why did he stress casual clothing?

7

With the onset of summer, Piper's schedule switched entirely to day shifts. That's when the store contracted with local chefs to showcase their specialties by holding courses on and off the premises. This change worked for two reasons: first, because these sessions were wildly popular with the public and second, it freed Piper up to help in the bakery and handle the increase in special orders.

With three graduation and two wedding cakes on top of the usual birthday cakes to prepare she went in early. Expressly responsible for the specialty orders Piper wasn't expected to help with regular bakery duties like rolls, breads, and pastries. Those were Joy's department but now at least she had someone to chat with while she worked. There was less pressure and more camaraderie.

She worked steadily, sparing only enough time to eat a yogurt so that she'd be done and out of the store by three-thirty. But by the time she stumbled exhausted into her apartment at a quarter to four the only thing she wanted to do was take a long hot shower and sack out on the couch for the rest of the night. She could see herself nodding off early because she wasn't used to setting her alarm, especially not at that ungodly hour.

Still dragging afterwards she seriously considered calling Chad and canceling. She was drying her hair when his call came and she got an unpleasant surprise. It was his voice on the line that revived her and not the shower.

"We can pick you up or you can meet us at our house, your choice," he said.

"Why don't I come over there?" It would be easier to call it a night if she drove herself.

He gave her directions.

They lived in a newer high-end development with graceful curving streets and intimate cul-de-sacs branching off in every direction. It would be easy to get lost in here because, though the styles of the individual houses varied from one to the next, they were all understated and tasteful. Every single yard looked professionally landscaped and obsessively maintained. The neighborhood was, for lack of a better description, a suburban utopia. Even the dogs she saw on leashes walked regally in front of their power-walking owners. It was kind of eerie. She should have just met them somewhere. Forget it, she should have cancelled. Who lives like this?

The Thomas house looked like all the others, not necessarily by design but it certainly met the standards of the neighborhood. It was sandstone neutral, the siding and bricks perfectly coordinated. The landscaping was beautiful and, dare she think it, spotless? Spotless. Who ever heard of spotless shrubbery? Yet, there it was. Very tidy, not a bike or ball left in the wrong place. Didn't kids make messes and leave their stuff everywhere? She certainly did when she was young. She heard about it constantly.

She pulled into their driveway, careful not to block the car parked in the open garage in case they were actually going somewhere. For all she knew they'd be hanging out and eating pizza delivery—expensive pizza delivery probably.

Piper tugged her keys out of the ignition and was just reaching for her door handle when the driver's door flew open and Kenny barked impatiently, "It's about time! We've been waiting forever."

Stunned, she climbed out of the car and stumbled over her apology. "Really? I'm sorry about that." Okay, maybe this was a huge mistake. She should tell the little brat to piss off and go back home.

Before she could do anything of the sort Missy flounced out of the house and stared in open admiration at Piper's purse.

"You brought your purse? I'm going to bring mine too!"

Missy spun to go get hers but her father stopped her at the

door. "No purses." He looked over his daughter's head at Piper and said, "I don't recommend it. Can you get by with just your I.D. and maybe a few dollars?"

"I suppose so," she answered slowly. "Care to tell me what we're doing?"

He shook his head and gave her a cryptic smile. "It's a surprise— for all of you."

"And it's driving me crazy," Kenny groaned.

"Am I dressed okay?" Piper asked. *He* certainly was. His worn jeans looked touchable and soft and unfortunately hugged him in all the right places. The simple clean t-shirt was much easier to deal with.

Chad looked Piper over appreciatively. He grinned when he came to her pastel tennis shoes. "You're perfect."

His warm assessment made her blush.

"Bathrooms, now or we're not leaving," Chad announced, waving the kids back into the house.

Both kids bolted inside, breaking off in different directions.

Chad turned back to her. "I strongly recommend you consider visiting the facilities too."

Piper's first impulse was to decline the need but then she thought there was probably a good reason he brought it up. No way did she want to get caught out somewhere and ruin everyone's fun because she brushed the suggestion aside.

Piper sighed as she followed him in. "Point the way."

"The master's available," he said, the single raised eyebrow he gave her implying so much more. "It's upstairs, the door on the right. You'll find it."

Without even turning, she knew his eyes lingered on her as she climbed.

The plush queen bed dominated the space and drew her eye immediately. She shook her head and snorted softly because it was flawlessly made, the comforter evenly spread over the top so that the overhang was precise on every side. Piper pictured her unmade bed at home and how inviting it was. This one begged to be photographed, not dived into. Pity because it really was a gorgeous bedroom set. She particularly liked the contrasting inlay of darker wood running around the edges of the lighter pieces. The beautiful television cabinet was probably her favorite and the focal point of the room, aside from the massive bed of course. Her eyes swept over the bed again and she wondered which side Chad slept on. Maybe he was like her, taking his half out of the middle. Whoa there, not a train of thought she wanted to follow. Pushing Chad and his bed out of her head, she slowed as she walked past the six-drawer dresser with mirror. Other than some framed pictures of the kids, the top was bare. Piper was sorely tempted to open a drawer or two but, catching her reflection in the glass, knew she couldn't do it.

She found the master bathroom was coordinated to seamlessly blend with the bedroom and like the rest, it was immaculate. This guy needed another hobby. Piper chuckled at the thought of him wearing rubber gloves and holding a toilet brush as she tugged down her jeans and sat. Turning her head she found herself admiring the large glassed-in shower for two—with seat. Probably not smart to venture there either.

Whether she appreciated it or not her curiosity got the better of her in the bathroom. After washing her hands Piper took a quick peek in Chad's medicine cabinet, relieved to find there was nothing interesting in it. The vanity however, was a different story. There was a faint cosmetic dusting on the bottom of the upper drawer and beneath a forgotten bag of cotton balls she found a compact of birth control pills.

Holding her breath she picked it up. After an uneasy pause she opened it to find over half the pills were gone. Peering at the expiration date stamped in the plastic she blinked when she realized the prescription was years out of date. Tucking the contraceptives back where she found them she shut the drawer silently. A heavy

Tara Mills

weight settled on her chest. Never had she felt so ashamed of herself. She had no business poking around and now that she had, she wasn't sure she wanted to think about what she found.

Everyone was waiting for her at the bottom of the stairs when Piper turned the corner and headed down. Chad brought Piper back to the kitchen and showed her a drawer where she could stow her purse while they were gone. Taking his advice, she grabbed just what she needed before they headed out to his car.

There are times when moods are as easy to perceive in the air as temperatures but it can still take a person by surprise. The shift in energy in the backseat was palpable as they drove to their secret destination, almost as if the kids suddenly sensed where they were going. Their hushed, excitable whispers made no sense to her at all but when she looked surreptitiously at Chad he was smiling, clearly enjoying their reaction. Without a word Chad pulled into the right turn lane and then Piper saw the Ferris wheel glimmering on the edge of the traveling carnival set up in the South Haven Mall parking lot and it all made sense.

The kids erupted in the back seat at the sight, their excited shrieks shrill and deafening. Piper winced and covered her ears.

"Hey! *Hey!*" Chad yelled over the noise. "Settle down."

"Thank you, Daddy!" Missy cried.

"Yeah, thanks, Dad," Kenny said, almost overcome with emotion.

Chad pulled into an empty space and shut off the engine. "You're welcome." He turned in his seat to look at them. "Now, listen up. We all stick together here. Got it?"

The kids nodded, absolutely sincere but once out of the car it was apparent he was asking too much. Even with shorter legs they still outdistanced the adults.

"Hurry!" they yelled back.

"I'm not sure I can handle a lot of spinning but I'm willing to ride a few things if you're game," he said, tucking his keys in his front pocket.

Piper grinned. "I'll give it a shot."

Okay, she had her answer anyway. This was definitely not a date. Now maybe she could relax and enjoy herself.

Chad stopped at the ticket booth and bought several long strands then handed them out.

The kids, poised to run, were startled when Chad clapped his hands on their shoulders and held them in place. He bent down and looked them right in the eyes. "One more time, we stay together or we go home right now."

Both kids nodded automatically, fighting desperately to see the action behind him.

He let them go and handed a string of tickets to Piper. "Keep those handy. I have a feeling we're gonna need them soon."

"So do I."

They both turned at Missy's gasp of delight and saw her take off for a ride called the Picnic Parade. Kenny ran after her and caught her by the hand, jerking her back.

"Don't waste your time," he said in disgust. "That's a kiddie ride."

Clearly conflicted, Missy let her brother drag her back but not without casting one last look of longing over her shoulder at the glossy ladybug, the shiny green inchworm, and the brilliant blue dragonfly before they were lost behind the moving crowd of fairgoers.

"Now, there!" Kenny stopped unexpectedly and pointed out the giant octopus, its eight arms rising and falling, the cars on the ends of each tentacle spinning rapidly as the entire contraption twirled. "That's what I'm talking about."

There was no way the kids could ride that monster without an adult escort. Chad could see the height restrictions even from here. He turned to Piper and shrugged apologetically.

She nodded. "Yeah, I figured. This is why you asked me to come along. You didn't want to ride all these things twice. Admit it."

Chad laughed. "Nah, that's just a side benefit."

Piper looked at the kids. "Okay, who's riding with me?"

"I am!" announced Missy. They all went to join the line of teenagers.

It struck Piper while they waited that their little foursome could easily be mistaken for just another family here tonight. Amused at first, Piper's smile froze when she realized she didn't exactly know how she felt about that. What a disturbing thought!

Chad had his own worries as he watched the ride. He wasn't kidding when he admitted that he had issues with spinning. The thought of possibly tossing his cookies in front of everyone, especially Piper, was too horrifying to contemplate.

Kenny saw his dad's grave expression and understood perfectly. He leaned in close and whispered, "Don't worry, Dad. I never get a good car."

Chad turned to consider his son, surprised that his apprehension was so transparent. Chuckling at himself he gave his son a playful elbow. Kenny elbowed him back.

Piper watched their interplay, not understanding what prompted it but charmed just the same. She turned to Missy. "Are you scared?"

"Are you?"

"No way. I love rides almost as much as Kenny does." She bent down and peered at Missy. "So are you scared?"

Missy blushed. "Maybe a little."

"Tell you what, you can hold my hand if you want. How does that sound?"

"Good."

Kenny's prediction was right of course, much to his disappointment, though he was the only one complaining afterwards that it was too tame. Piper on the other hand, thoroughly enjoyed herself and her unfettered excitement infected Missy too. Piper looked over at Chad and her mouth twitched. The poor guy looked a little peaked.

"You gonna make it?" she asked, feeling a twinge of sympathy.

"I'm good," Chad said calmly, his flu-like pallor beside the point.

Moving along afterwards with a spring in her step and a bouncing kid on either side, Piper enthusiastically joined their critique of the ride while Chad followed along, shaking his head and smiling at the threesome.

Being tallest, Chad spotted the Tilt-O-Whirl seconds before Piper did. She caught the look on his face and nodded back, understanding he might need more time to recover from the last ride. Working in tandem they tried to maneuver the kids in a different direction before they saw the ride too but Kenny thwarted them.

"We gotta!" he said, cutting towards it.

Piper shrugged at Chad. "I tried."

"I know."

"Come on!" Kenny waved them over.

Missy ran to join him.

Catching up, Chad asked Kenny doubtfully. "You sure about this one?"

"Oh yeah."

Missy nodded excitedly. "You can sit by me, Dad."

"Actually," he hedged. "I think I'm going to sit this one out."

"No. You can't!" She gave her dad a desperate, pleading look.

Chad turned to Piper. "Well I'm not going alone."

"Who said I wasn't going?"

He stared at her, processing this surprising turn of events. "Then why were you helping me steer them away from it?"

She gave Chad a long look. "Gee, I wonder."

"I said, I'm fine."

"Uh huh."

"Come on, Daddy," said Missy, reaching for his hand.

"No," he finally said. "You three go ahead. I'll wait down here."

Piper smiled wickedly at Chad, then turned to the kids. "Wasn't it his rule that we all stick together?"

They both nodded firmly and Chad shook his head at Piper. "That's low."

She grinned back. "Then we'll vote on it. Who's in favor of riding the Tilt-O-Whirl?"

Three right hands shot into the air.

"It's not scary, honest. You're going to like it," Missy said, giving Chad the hard sell.

"I've ridden on Tilt-O-Whirls before," he said.

"Then you know how fun they are," Kenny said, effectively closing down the arguments.

Chad threw up his hands and followed them up the steps. It was easier than digging in his heels and useless to try and explain the difference between the slower controlled spin of the Octopus and the sudden whips this ride was going to send them on.

The kids raced along the platform and dove into their car of choice, each claiming an end and leaving the adults the center of the curved seat.

Sitting rather cozily Chad pressed his knee against Piper's. She turned and he asked, "I don't have to worry about my lap here do I?"

"Not likely. Do I?"

He patted his solid stomach. "Empty."

Piper eyed him skeptically and sighed. Oh yeah, this was going to be great.

As soon as their car hurtled into its first insane spin both kids went into action, throwing their little bodies back and forth and leaning aggressively to send them spinning into the next at full speed. Chad and Piper had no time to plan counter measures in advance but somehow they inadvertently managed to nullify a lot of what the kids were trying to do anyway.

At the end, as their car rolled to a shaky stop Kenny said, "We have to do it again, Dad. You messed us up."

Yet despite all Kenny's grumbling, while the ride was in motion there were plenty of gasps and squeals coming from all of them.

Once Chad's feet touched solid ground he made an alternate suggestion. "Maybe Piper and I should just watch from the side. You two can show us how it's supposed to be done."

"Fine. Come on, Missy."

The line was short so they were able to get right back on again without waiting.

Watching them as the ride got underway it was obvious the kids knew what they were doing. Their car spun like a spool and the kids screamed and laughed ecstatically every time it shot off into another tight loop.

Chad turned away, looking a little pale. "I can't watch. I swear it's making me nauseous. Good thing I didn't feed them first."

"I don't think they're the ones we need to worry about. No, don't look. I'll tell you when it's over."

"Thanks."

Piper chuckled to herself, amused at this unexpected side of him. She kind of liked it. No one should be too perfect.

The kids bounded down the steps with no apparent side effects, already planning to ride the Tilt-O-Whirl again later.

The next two rides they wandered by looked so insane they belonged in a category all by themselves. Even Piper refused to ride when Kenny pressed her and no amount of begging would change her mind. He knew enough not to bother with his father. He had to let it go but he didn't have to like it.

The last of the large rides was an old fashioned scrambler. When Chad saw it, his face lit up. He herded them into line. "I love these things!"

"You sure you're up to this?"

"This I can handle," he assured her.

Piper laughed, noticing the similarities between father and son as they eyed the contraption.

They paired off by sex once again and when they were let into the fenced area Kenny chose a car that would race right at Piper and Missy, just barely missing them as they sped around in circles.

Piper pulled the abbreviated door closed in front of them and threw the bolt. She turned to the little girl beside her. "Don't worry if you slide into me."

"I won't slide," said Missy confidently.

The first couple of circuits were nice and easy and everyone laughed and waved as they passed each other but by the third hurtling pass they were all too absorbed in their own personal struggles to let go of the bars and wave let alone notice the other two as they careened by. Missy clung to the grab bar fighting to stay on her side but she couldn't do it. Over and over again she slammed into Piper, every collision making them laugh even harder. Finally, Piper lifted her arm and pulled Missy against her and they sat back and enjoyed the rest of the ride like conjoined twins.

The girls caught up with the guys afterwards right outside the gate and they took an immediate vote to see if they should ride the Scrambler again. It was unanimous. All four ran around to rejoin the line.

"I'm riding with Piper this time," Chad announced, stepping to her side.

8

The minor change in the seating arrangement was no big deal to the kids but Piper needed to give herself another silent pep talk.

You can do this. There's nothing to be afraid of—honestly. Chad's not going to make a move on you in public and especially not in front of his kids. It's cool. Everything's cool. No worries.

Still, when their turn came to claim their seats Piper had more outward calm than inner. Chad caught the door and held it open, waiting for her to climb in first. There was an awkward moment when he offered his hand to assist her up but Piper didn't see it until after she grabbed the edge of the seat instead. He dropped his hand and followed her in.

Trying to get comfortable, Piper was highly sensitive to the disturbing lack of wiggle room with two adults riding together. Seeing how edgy the close quarters made her, Chad stretched his arm out behind Piper to create more room. It didn't exactly calm her.

Piper shot a wary look at the hand draped just behind her left shoulder. There was a hint of hysteria in her voice when she tried to joke it off. "Pretty slick, I see where this is going."

"Relax," Chad said, overlooking her suspicions. "I'm just trying to save my shoulder and give you a little more space. But, if you feel a sudden urge to throw yourself at me anyway well, I won't complain."

There was no point in making an issue of it now. Besides, if she had real qualms about riding with him she should have spoken up sooner, before she parked her fanny next to him.

The clutch released and the ride began its first slow easy circuit and Piper smiled, already anticipating the fun she was about to have. When the kids passed they both waved back just as enthusiastically. It was the third circuit around that changed the playbook on her. First Piper was crowding Chad. Then she was sliding into him, ramming him repeatedly with her hip as she fought to maintain a respectable distance.

Laughing harder and harder at the futility of the effort, Piper wore herself out and Chad shook his head with amusement and dropped his arm around her, holding her close to his side. Only then was Piper able to admit defeat and finally relax and enjoy herself.

The way her emotions were whipping around reminded her of the arms that sent the cars careening at each other. She was breathless, delighting in the thrill of the ride and trembling because there was another body, a seriously hot body, hard against her. She was practically in his lap but Chad didn't seem to mind. Every time the kids shrieked past them they cheered. Piper couldn't remember laughing so hard.

Chad could feel Piper's breast pressed against him and, as embarrassing as it would be to admit this aloud, he pressed back, loving how her nipple came out to make his silent acquaintance. He tried not to look at it but it was there, right there. What was a guy supposed to do? At least he was discreet about it.

He loved how Piper waved wildly at the kids whenever they met in passing. He grinned like a fool when she yelled, "Hello again!" to the people standing outside the circular fence as they shot right at them. She was so open and free with her smiles and laughter. Would she be that way with her love too? Imagining it, he could already see himself falling for her in a big way.

Like all amusements, it wasn't nearly long enough. As the ride began to slow Chad saw his magical window closing. He turned to Piper without a word and tipped her chin up, giving her a gentle kiss.

Piper's lashes fluttered in surprise as he eased back. He smiled, grateful and encouraged that she hadn't pushed him away.

"Sorry," he said simply. "I just wanted to avoid any awkwardness later. Is that okay?"

"Um, yeah, fine," Piper stammered.

Once the cars stopped Chad turned to open the door, effectively hiding his face from Piper but when he climbed out and turned, she was bowled over by the warmth in his expressive eyes and the intimate smile he gave her. Now, this time when he offered his hand to assist her, Piper needed it.

Leaving the rides behind them, they stopped to buy corn dogs and drinks then set off to wander through the midway and watch the games.

The kids tugged them over to a fishing game, eager to try their luck. Unfortunately Missy lost interest because she couldn't control her line so she drifted off with Piper to look at the next booth while Kenny went on to win a fuzzy yellow fish.

Chad had his eye on the Bottle Ball booth directly across from them. He gave Piper a nudge and nodded in that direction. "Care to take me on?"

The confident jock was back. Feeling pretty confident herself Piper agreed. "You're on."

They crossed over to the booth and Chad plunked money down on the counter. The barker gave them three balls apiece in return.

"Be my guest," Chad offered, clearly not worried about the competition. He tossed a ball lightly into the air and caught it again and again without even looking.

"Showoff." There was nothing Piper wanted to do more than wipe that cocky smirk off of his face. "Fine."

She picked up her first ball and yanked her arm back, sending the ball on a wild flight into the far corner of the stall.

The momentary hush of astonishment was followed immediately by a burst of laughter. Chad, Kenny, and Missy all lost it, and much to Piper's chagrin, even the attendant was struggling to hold it in.

Catching Piper's cool look, Chad composed himself and brushed at his eyes. "That has to be the girliest throw I've ever seen."

"For your information," Piper said tightly, "I am a girl."

Chad grinned, looking her over. "I noticed."

"You think you're such hot stuff, why don't you show me what you've got then?"

He moved in close and teased softly, "Watch it or I might take you literally."

She elbowed him in his seven-minute abs. "Just throw the blasted ball."

He winked. "Coward." Tossing the ball from hand to hand a few times first, Chad finally drew back his arm. The ball flew so fast Piper lost sight of it but the throw was dead accurate and sent all the bottles clattering.

"Awesome!" the kids cheered.

"Lucky shot," said Piper, both amused and alarmingly aroused.

Chad waved her forward and Piper picked up her next ball. She turned her head and crinkled her nose at him for good measure then faced forward again while he laughed.

Pursing her lips, she considered her options. Since he was going to laugh anyway she might as well. She stepped back just enough so she could lob it underhanded and was as amazed as everyone else when she actually knocked several bottles down.

Chad beamed at her. "That was ugly but effective. Nice job."

When they finally moved on Missy was holding a fuzzy purple monkey and Kenny had added a bright orange frog to his tacky collection. Chad offered to win Piper something larger than the backscratcher she won for herself but she declined, actually quite happy with her prize.

Chad hoped they could get by the Tilt-O-Whirl without stopping but once Kenny and Missy saw it that was no longer possible. After a hurried search through everyone's pockets they were able to pool together just enough tickets for the kids to take one final ride.

Piper and Chad took temporary custody of their toys while the kids climbed into a car.

Chad looked a bit unsure about this last ride. "They just ate. This might not be pretty. I don't know if I can watch."

"They look hearty to me."

"Let's hope our luck holds."

Piper laughed and he smiled at her.

Suddenly self-conscious, Piper looked away and focused on smoothing out a rough seam on Missy's monkey instead. Her eyes drifted up as the Tilt-O-Whirl began to circle. "This has to be one of the stranger first dates I've ever been on."

He smiled at that. "Would you be open to a second?"

"That depends. Am I going to have bed spins afterwards?" She was teasing but the smoldering look in his eyes shifted the mood instantly.

"If I kiss you right," said Chad.

Piper's stomach did a flip and before her brain could catch up, she said, "Then I might consider a second."

9

Casting covert looks at Chad while he drove, Piper silently chastised herself. What was she doing? What was she thinking? One hot stud waltzes in and she's ready to scrap her newfound independence? She was pathetic. She had to get out of here, put some distance between them before she was sucked even further into his orbit.

And yet, when Chad pulled the car into the garage and said, "Don't hurry off," she relented.

Feeling utterly ridiculous when she did it, but not wanting to seem like the foregone conclusion she apparently was, Piper casually checked the time first. "I suppose I can stay a little while."

The kids bolted into the house. Chad called after them, "Missy, you get the shower first. Ken, get your pajamas ready so you can jump in next." Chad caught the door for Piper and stood back, following her in.

They could hear Kenny groaning all the way upstairs when they walked into the kitchen.

"Take a seat." Chad waved her over to the other side of the counter.

He went to the refrigerator and pulled open the door while Piper slid out a stool and hopped up.

"Let's see, we have iced tea, fruit punch, milk, or a nice bottle of white I've been saving. Name your poison."

"I'll have what you're having."

He straightened with a smile, the bottle of wine in his hand. "I was hoping you'd say that."

Piper took a minute to look around the kitchen while he got a couple of glasses out of the cabinet. "You have a beautiful home. How long have you lived here?"

"Nine years."

He rummaged around in a drawer until he found his corkscrew then went after the cork, pulling it free with a pleasant pop. He lined up the glasses and poured. "We moved in just after we found out Chelsea was pregnant."

Piper wanted to ask, oh boy did she want to ask but she hesitated. Chad saw it.

"You want to know where my wife is but you don't want to bring it up right?" He slid a glass towards her.

Piper nodded. It was easier than admitting it out loud.

"Chelsea died in a car accident five years ago." He took a sip of wine then studied the liquid in his glass thoughtfully before going on. "She'd just dropped the kids off at daycare. From what I understand she was merging onto the interstate when a driver in the far left lane barreled across traffic in order to hit the exit ramp. He caused a five-car pile-up. It wasn't pretty. They needed the Jaws of Life to cut her free. She died in the ambulance on the way to the hospital."

Chad stopped talking and stared at Piper for a minute, a haunted man. "I could have lost all of them. The car seats in the back were completely destroyed. If you can be lucky when something so bad happens, I guess I was because it could have happened before she dropped the kids off, not after."

"I'm so sorry." Her heart ached for him.

He gave her a helpless smile. "Thanks. I wasn't sure I'd be able to pull through, but I had to. Kenny and Missy needed me." He let out a quick burst of air and shook his head slowly. "And I needed them. They were so young. They forced me to focus. I can't say that I didn't have some really rough patches when all I wanted to do was withdraw into grief. I did. But young twins won't let you stay there and brood." He took a deep swallow and continued. "It hasn't been easy but we've made the best of a bad situation and come out closer than we might have been otherwise."

"I can see you're close."

He was ready to turn the conversation, very ready. He lifted the bottle and used it to wave her towards the doorway. "Let's go into the living room. It's more comfortable."

Piper dropped to her feet and followed him. They took a seat on the sofa, facing in, their knees bent, almost touching over the center cushion.

"How about you? You told my mom you aren't from the area. What's your story?"

"I'm from Martin Heights."

"Sure, three hours west."

"Right. Anyway, I reached a point where I needed to make a fresh start, put a little distance between me and my ex. He has a way of turning up. You might say he's my bad penny."

A moment of clarity hit him. "No wonder you were so edgy when I stopped you in the parking lot."

She saw that he had the wrong impression and hurried to correct it. "No, Mick never hurt me physically. His problem, which became my problem, was that he was a living tar pit. The longer we were together the more exhausting it was for me. He never meant to wear me down, he was just being Mick. He's got an incurable Peter Pan complex. Didn't want to grow up or be responsible. He had no problem indulging in the fun side of adulthood but he didn't stay around to pick up the check or clean up after the party."

"So you divorced him?"

Piper shook her head. "Didn't have to, we weren't married. I moved out. Unfortunately it didn't stop Mick from keeping in touch. He knows how to work me when he needs something, especially cash, and since I have a habit of taking on his responsibilities I needed to make myself scarce."

"And three hours away is working?"

"So far. Of course he doesn't know where I am."

He looked at her thoughtfully. "Then I need to ask. Why

have you been so prickly towards me? If you didn't find me physically dangerous…"

Her quick head shake and smile reassured him.

"Okay, so why did you threaten to blast me with pepper spray?"

"Mace," Piper corrected with a laugh. "I'm not sure. My best guess is that I was lashing out from embarrassment. You did make me look ridiculous in front of my class."

"I made you look ridiculous, how?"

"You know how."

"How?" he pressed, peering expectantly into her eyes.

"You distracted me and everyone knew it. Why wouldn't I be angry?"

He grinned. "Well, I thought it was fantastic. Do you know I blew off a dinner party my best friends were throwing—for me apparently—when I saw you?"

"You did? You weren't registered for the class?"

His smile deepened. "No. We're drinking my hostess gift right now as a matter of fact. It's the reason I went to the store in the first place."

"Wow. Are they mad at you?"

"They were. Apparently it was a set-up and I left them hanging."

"And you didn't know?"

"Right again." He reached for the bottle of wine and topped each glass before setting it back on the coffee table.

"Huh." Piper smiled and took a sip. "I owe you an apology. I've been a real bitch. I didn't want to like you."

"Apology accepted." Chad tapped his glass against hers. "To a fresh start."

Time moved sluggishly while they sipped, eyes locked. The space between them felt weighted and as it collapsed into itself it drew them in too until they were so close their breath mingled. The faint smell of the crisp wine seemed to be the only thing resistant to the pull. Piper's lashes drooped, suddenly heavy and just when she felt the barest tickle of his lips on hers a sound as loud as a bowling ball crashing down the stairs jolted them both back to reality. They sprang apart guiltily right before Kenny stormed into the room.

"Missy's not out yet!"

Chad looked at Piper, his expression a mixture of disappointment and apology. "Will you excuse me a second?"

"Sure."

Chad followed his son upstairs and knocked on the bathroom door.

There was panic in Missy's voice. "Don't come in!"

"Honey, Kenny needs to shower too. Can you hurry it up?"

She unlocked the door and pulled it open. She was holding her slippers against her chest and there was a comb sticking out from her wet hair.

Chad smiled at her. "Can I help?"

Missy nodded and they moved aside so Kenny could take possession of the bathroom. The boy slammed the door between them. Still standing in the hall Chad eased the comb free then carefully worked at the tangles one by one. He cursed himself for forgetting to buy the conditioner. He'd pick some up tomorrow.

When Chad walked back through the archway and into the living room the pleasure Piper felt was so intense it terrified her. Shaken, she downed the rest of her wine and bolted to her feet, setting the empty glass on the coffee table.

"I'm sorry but I really need to get going. My work schedule is changing and I've got an early day tomorrow," she said hurriedly, practically stumbling over her excuses.

Chad's face fell but he didn't pressure her. "Okay, I'll get your purse."

She followed him back to the kitchen and waited impatiently while he pulled it out of the drawer. Handing it over Chad followed

Piper back down the hall to the foyer. She wanted nothing more at this particular moment than to put some distance between them, fast, before it was too late.

Her pulse quickened when she realized his intentions. "You don't have to walk me out."

"Of course I do."

Piper didn't argue but she wanted to. When they reached her car she grabbed the door handle but Chad reached up and put his palm flat against the window, holding it closed. Startled, she turned to face him, uncomfortably aware of just how close he was standing to her.

10

"Listen, I should have thanked you for tonight. I had a nice time." Piper's lame attempt at defusing the tension was obvious.

Chad nodded, his heavenly eyes considering her thoughtfully. Nervous perspiration started to trickle out of her pores. "And you have two really great kids. Say good-night for me, would you?"

He nodded again. "Why are you running, Piper?" His voice was so soft, so low it was almost a whisper. He leaned towards her, forcing her to look up at him.

Her eyes darted to the right when she tried to deny it. "I'm not."

"Oh, that was convincing." He chuckled. "Can we cut the bullshit? You do something to me and clearly I'm affecting you. I think we owe it to ourselves to explore it—together."

She couldn't even formulate a coherent thought when Chad was practically touching her, crowding her like this. He was much too close, too warm. The intoxicating smell of him insinuated itself into her nose like a drug and pumped her already careening blood flow even faster through her body.

His control astounded her. She was firing flames out her fingertips and he was the definition of cool. Slowly he tilted her chin up and lowered his mouth to hers. Piper found herself responding, unable to do anything else. Then he pulled back but his eyes still held her, a captured thing and she only had time enough for one quick breath before he dove again and swallowed the breath right out of her.

This kiss was harder, more demanding and Piper rode the curve of the car like a chamois cloth as he bent her backwards. Chad's body molded itself to hers, pressed tight, and his fingers combed up through her hair.

When he eventually eased back, Chad brought Piper with him, returning her to an upright position. Her legs buckled.

"Whoa there," he said, catching her.

He pulled her door open and Piper dropped weakly onto the seat and stared up at him with glazed eyes.

"Where are your keys?" Chad's question barely penetrated her mental fog.

Piper pulled them from her purse and started the engine.

Chad watched her with growing concern. "Hey, are you going to be all right?"

She nodded, completely rattled and not entirely sure what he just asked.

"Open your window. I think you need the air." He smiled and closed the door for her. Piper lowered the window and looked up at him, her confusion finally beginning to clear.

He leaned in. "Be safe. I'll call you."

"Okay," she mumbled.

Piper stared at her steering wheel in distress. She'd lost her marbles! Where the hell was she going again? Oh yeah, home, she needed to get home. She hoped she could find her way back from here. She couldn't believe how Chad completely rearranged her gray matter with that kiss.

Chad was relieved when Piper managed to back out of his driveway without a mishap. By the time she reached the corner and her brakes lit up he knew she would be fine. He turned back to the house with a satisfied chuckle. *Oh honey, look out. I've been saving up.*

It was after ten the next morning and as unbelievable as it seemed, Alice was back walking the aisles of the Ritz Grocery Store, otherwise known to the locals as Klein's. This time she went without Chad. She was on a mission, to interfere if necessary, on his behalf. He didn't need to hear about it. Not if she played her cards right anyway.

Her eyes were keen as she scoped the produce section first then moved on to meats in search of the elusive woman. Just when she was beginning to consider scrapping the whole effort as a momentary lapse of judgment she spotted Piper standing behind glass, decorating what was going to be a three-tiered cake. She was applying very realistic frosting violets to the butter cream so it took her a few minutes to notice that she had an audience.

"Hello, Victoria!" Alice greeted her with a wave.

"It's Piper," she said with a laugh.

"Right, right."

"Hang on," Piper called out and gave the pastry bag in her hand a couple more twists and bent to finish the row she was working on.

Finally done, she stepped out from behind the glass and adjusted the neck of her apron. She gave Alice an uncertain smile across the top of the case.

"You do beautiful work," said Alice.

"Thank you." Piper took a deep breath. "Listen, I think I know what you're doing here so let me save you a little time by telling you that I've already been out with Chad, the whole family actually."

Alice beamed, the impulse to drum ecstatically on the glass case almost getting the better of her. "Really—how was it?"

"Different. Nice." Piper hid a bashful smile behind her hand.

Encouraged, Alice said, "You could do a lot worse."

Piper laughed. "Any mother would say that."

"True, but would they really believe it?"

"I wouldn't know."

"I would. Most mothers love their children unconditionally but we aren't completely blind to who they are, faults and all."

"Surely you're not suggesting Chad has faults?" Piper teased.

"Oh honey, we'd need to grab a lunch if you want to discuss

him in detail." Alice laughed. "I'm just kidding. But seriously, Chad's a good catch."

"Maybe we *should* have lunch. You might be a safer bet than your son."

"I wouldn't count on it." Alice gave Piper an understanding look. "He unsettles you, doesn't he?"

"Big time."

"You know, his father had the same effect on me. Threw me loopy. I feel for you." She reached across the case and patted Piper's hand. "I'm Alice, by the way, Alice Thomas. I'm in the book. Call if you want, I have a sympathetic ear. But I warn you now, I'm biased."

"But of course."

"Just so we understand one another."

At the end of her shift Piper pulled off her apron and hung it up then went to work on the kinks in her lower back, finally rolling her shoulders to ease the tight muscles. She was just stretching out her neck when the phone on the back wall rang.

"I'm off the clock," she reminded Joy, grabbing her purse.

Joy rolled her eyes and caught the phone. "Bakery. Yeah, just a second." She held out the phone with a smug grin. "For you."

Piper snapped her fingers and grumbled all the way back to take the foul thing. Visions of her nice soothing shower were evaporating fast. Joy looked at her curiously as she handed the phone over.

"This is Piper."

"Good, I caught you. Come over."

"Who is this?"

"Chad."

To her annoyance her knees went weak on her. "What did you just say?"

"It's Chad."

"No, before that."

"Oh, come over."

"Why? I was planning to hit the lake."

"I have another idea."

"Why am I not surprised?"

"Hey, I can guarantee you'll be perfectly safe and we'll have two pint-sized chaperones again."

"I've heard that one before. Listen, I should probably tell you now that I'm not exactly the family fun type."

"Did you have a good time last night?"

She screwed up her face before reluctantly answering, "Yes."

"There you go. Wear a bathing suit."

"A bathing suit?"

"Dress for me—not the kids."

She could picture his grin from here. "Right," she said with a snort then smiled anyway.

He laughed. "See you soon, Piper."

He hung up before she could raise any more objections. Hanging up on her end, Piper cursed him, herself, and fate as she headed out to her car, so distracted she completely missed Joy's wide-eyed stare following her.

11

Thirty minutes later Piper was still fuming but committed to the idea as she rummaged through her dresser drawer at home.

"Dress for me," she muttered, throwing her tasteful one piece and the matching sarong onto the bed. She felt rebellious when she slipped into it knowing she had a very sexy little number buried in her underwear drawer that he'd appreciate so much more. Then she realized how silly she was behaving and laughed at herself.

Chad had balls—she had to give him that. Not that she was in any hurry to see them. Crap. There she goes again, straying in directions she really shouldn't. That nonsense had to stop.

"This is it," Piper coached herself as she pulled into the driveway. "You're an adult. You're in control. Nothing you don't want to happen has to happen."

Bucked up by her pep talk she got out and turned to shut the car door. That's when Kenny leaped from the bushes with his Super Soaker and blasted her in the back, drenching her with ice cold water.

It would be hard to say what went higher, Piper's scream or her startled leap into the air. When she returned to her feet she whipped around with a, "You little— " but the kid was already rounding the corner of the garage.

Piper took off after the little monster, visions of revenge spurring her on.

Kenny hit the backyard mere inches ahead of Piper's grasping hand when, to the surprise of both, Kenny went spinning up into the air, his weapon arcing out of his hands and landing in the grass several feet away.

The boy was suddenly perched across his dad's shoulder like a flailing airplane, all hands and kicking feet.

Chad turned to Piper and she thought he was going to come to his son's defense but she was wrong.

"Going somewhere?" Chad asked Kenny ominously. He looked at Piper. "He nailed you, didn't he?"

"You could say that." Piper turned and showed her back, pulling the clammy fabric away from her bare skin.

"I think a little torture is in order," Chad said with a sinister chuckle.

"Torture?" Piper asked.

"The tickle treatment."

Kenny started laughing and squirming. "Dad, no! I'll pee. Dad!"

Taking the warning seriously Chad relented and looked at Piper. "Fine. Piper, you choose the consequences."

Following Chad's lead she rubbed her hands together wickedly. "It has to be good."

He grinned. "Naturally."

Struck by sudden inspiration, Piper pulled her purse around from her shoulder and went rummaging. Both Kenny and Chad went momentarily still, watching her curiously. Then she produced her lipstick and Ken's struggles got louder and more desperate.

Piper winked at Chad. "See this? This lipstick is hot pink, a pink so bright you need sunglasses just to put it on. I think Kenny should have to ride his bike up and down the street three times so that all his friends get a chance to see how pretty he is wearing it."

"No!" Kenny screamed in horror. His struggles shifted from desperate to violent.

Clearly it was time to calm him down before he accidentally hurt his dad. "Or," she said reasonably. "He can promise me no more sneak attacks or the lipstick comes out and I won't be merciful."

"Okay, okay, deal," Kenny agreed.

Piper was still brandishing her lipstick when Missy came through the screen door, her wide eyes fixed on the tube. "Can I wear lipstick?"

"No!" both adults answered together, Piper because she didn't want the natural peach to give her away and Chad because he just plain wasn't ready for his daughter to dabble in cosmetics yet.

"Now what do you say to Piper?" Chad asked his son.

"I'm sorry."

"You're forgiven," said Piper.

Chad flipped Kenny over and set him on his feet. The kid took off with a whoop of relief and his father turned to Piper with a warm smile. "Way to play ball."

She shrugged casually, quashing the impulse to beam like a drunken idiot at his approval. "Hey, I know how to tag."

"Come on up. I think the hamburgers are about ready to be flipped." He glanced back. "Why don't you take off that wet shirt and hang it on the railing there? Then we'll go inside and set you up properly. We've got beer, iced tea, a juice box maybe?"

"I'll take straight water if you've got it."

"It's our best seller." He headed up onto the deck.

Piper looked back at the yard and the net set up on the grass. "You play badminton?"

"A form of it anyway," he said with another one of those cryptic smiles of his. Chad lifted the cover of the grill and picked up his flipper. After a minute he closed the lid and frowned at Piper. "You're still wearing that wet shirt."

"Yeah, well…"

He chuckled, understanding perfectly. "Fine, if it makes you feel more comfortable you can borrow one of mine but eventually you're going to want to take it off."

"Is that right?"

"Mmm hmm."

"I'll take one of yours anyway."

Smirking, he pulled back the screen door. "After you." He followed her inside and pointed the way. "Laundry room is down on the left. You can't miss it. There should be a clean shirt by the dryer."

There were three stacks of folded clothes on the cabinet and no doubt about whose pile was whose. Piper went through Chad's and pulled out the first t-shirt she found. He was setting ketchup and mustard on a tray when she wandered outside to hang her shirt over the deck railing. Then she came back inside and leaned her hip against the counter.

Chad turned and nodded thoughtfully at her shirt of choice. "Gotta love Snoopy. You ready for that water?"

"Point me to the glasses."

"I've got it," he said opening an upper cabinet. He took it to the refrigerator and pressed the glass against the ice dispenser. The cubes were halfway up the glass when he stopped abruptly and turned with an apologetic shrug. "Ice?"

Piper laughed. "Sure, why not?"

"Whew. I thought I was gonna have to set these babies free."

"Return them to their natural habitat?"

"Not quite. I was thinking the drain in the sink."

"Seems a cruel way to dispose of them."

"I thought so, too."

He filled the glass with water then passed it to her before reaching into the fridge to get a cold beer. They went back out to the deck.

Piper dropped into one of the bouncy chairs while Chad checked on the burgers.

"Can I ask you something?" she said.

"Shoot."

"Why am I wearing a bathing suit?"

He glanced over his shoulder with a playful grin. "I wanted us to match?"

"Pardon?"

He turned and pulled his shirt up, flashing his swim shorts along with an edible eyeful of bare stomach, modestly furred of course. The flip comment she was about to make lodged in her throat and she needed a quick gulp of water to wash it down.

But Chad seemed to know what she was thinking, anyway. He winked and raised his bottle to his lips.

Piper rolled her eyes at him and tried not to stare at his Adam's apple but the way it dipped as he swallowed was utterly fascinating. It wasn't usually that obvious.

Chad lowered the bottle and turned his head, calling, "Hey you clowns! Front and center."

Missy and Kenny assembled on the grass in front of him.

"Is it time to eat?" Kenny asked hopefully.

"Just about, you know what to do."

The kids bounded up the steps and into the kitchen. Chad went to take the burgers off the heat.

"Can I help with anything?" Piper asked.

"They've got it covered. Missy does the tableware and Kenny's got the edibles."

Right on cue, Kenny came out carrying the tray with ketchup, mustard, buns, and chips. Missy followed with a stack of plates and napkins.

As soon as the kids claimed their favorite chairs Piper realized she would be facing their dad while she ate. To a normal person that would be no big deal but Piper had issues. Since childhood she'd been uncomfortable eating in front of people. It took her time to relax and not feel self-conscious. So she nibbled, snuck little bites into her mouth and tried to chew discretely. She never understood where this strange hypersensitive quirk came from yet it lived on. She settled onto a chair while Chad stood over the kids, helping them set up their plates. When he finally sat across from her she wondered how she would manage this. The night before wasn't an issue because they ate corn dogs while they walked so their attention was directed elsewhere. But this was a whole different situation, more intimate. She couldn't just pretend him away, especially if he watched her as he was wont to do.

Piper's fears were groundless. Though she felt Chad's gaze on her repeatedly, she didn't have a chance to stress over it because the kids monopolized the meal, hopping up and down in their seats and talking excitedly about their interests.

After supper, Piper overrode their objections that she was a guest and pitched in with cleanup. Once everything was put away they all returned to the deck and Chad offered Piper something a little more potent to drink. Piper chose to stick with water. Frankly it was too warm and she had doubts about her ability to handle herself under the influence. She didn't want to flirt with a repeat of last night. The last thing she needed in her life right now was a new lover. But she could sure use more friends. She hadn't realized until yesterday just how lonely she'd been since moving here. Joy was right, she needed to expand her social circle but that didn't mean she was interested in being friends with benefits. It would be a lot easier to remember that if her head was clear.

Kenny leaped over the steps to the grass beyond yelling, "Boys against the girls!"

"Yeah!" Missy bunny hopped down the steps after her brother.

The boy disappeared down the side yard to get the hose. They could hear the squeak squeak squeak of the spigot when he turned on the water.

Chad turned to Piper. "Do you remember what I said about your shirt?"

"Yes," she answered warily.

"Now would be a good time to take it off."

Before she could ask why he grabbed the bottom of his shirt and yanked it over his head, tossing it onto a chair.

Okay, he had her attention now. The pick-up line, "If I said you had a great body would you hold it against me?" popped into her head. Piper stared, overwhelmed by how casually he undressed and completely flummoxed by her sudden awareness of him. It was hard enough relaxing with Chad when there always seemed to be tension hovering between them but this display was hitting several inches below the belt.

It was a fortunate coincidence that a mere half second before Chad would have caught her salivating over his scrumptious physique Kenny came back dragging the hose and sprinkler. Chad turned that way instead, saving Piper from complete humiliation. She decided then and there that not only was Kenny forgiven for his sneak attack but she owed the kid—big.

The boy set the sprinkler on its edge, directly below the net, and waited for it to cycle back before setting it properly and dashing clear.

"It's ready!" he yelled.

Chad looked at Piper. "Come on then."

She studied the lawn. "We're going to play badminton under the sprinkler?"

"Yes and trust me, you're going to love it." His words, his eyes were loaded with innuendo.

Piper sighed and shifted a quarter turn before pulling her shirt up over her head. It made a handy screen for her blushes. This was not the time and this was certainly not the place to feel this level of arousal.

"Very nice," Chad said softly, sending seductive shivers skittering across her skin.

"I've got the racquets," Missy called up to her.

Piper turned to the girl with a grateful smile, tempted to give Missy a big hug for bringing her back to her senses.

"So are we going to play or what?" Piper asked tartly and waltzed down the steps and onto the grass with as much poise as she could muster.

Piper accepted the racquet Missy held out to her and took her position. "Now, take it easy on me because I haven't played this in years."

"Don't worry, we don't really keep score," Missy admitted.

"It's not really the point," Chad added across the net.

For a game that really wasn't a game at all it was still hilarious fun. Their goal seemed to be keeping the birdies in the air for as long as possible and anything ugly or balletic or downright crazy was permitted as long as they didn't let it hit the ground. They slid and skated across the wet grass falling time and time again until they were all drenched and speckled in mud.

If that didn't pose enough of a challenge for Piper there was the added difficulty of pretending to be immune to Chad's bare athletic body right in front of her. Then of course even more difficult was ignoring how Chad seemed to enjoy watching *her* bounce more than the birdie during their livelier volleys. Still, the sexual tension aside, Piper had a great time. Had they bothered to keep score, there was no question the boys would have kicked their butts.

Once the sun dropped below the tree line and the shadows lengthened they shut off the water. There was a noticeable drop in temperature now and they shivered as they traipsed into the house just ahead of a platoon of mosquitoes looking for a late meal.

Chad sent Piper back to the laundry room to find another set of dry clothes while the family scattered to their rooms to change. She was just coming out dressed in another of his shirts and a pair of his sweats when Chad came around the corner carrying their wet suits. She waited while he threw everything into the washer. Looking over his shoulder he held out his hand for her bathing suit too. Piper passed it to him. The machine was humming away when they returned to the kitchen.

That's when Chad finally noticed that Piper was shivering and her hair was still so wet it was dripping onto her shoulders.

Obviously upset he asked, "Wasn't there a towel in there?"

She shook her head. "But that's okay. I'm fine."

"No you're not. Wait right there."

Chad was back in a flash, holding open a large plush bath towel. She moved to take it from him but he shook his head and wrapped her in it himself, pinning her arms to her sides while he roughed her skin up and down and pressed the ends of her dripping hair between the layers.

Piper stood frozen, looking up at him until he stopped and dropped his head down to kiss her gently. He nuzzled her with his cheek, his nose, and Piper leaned into him, accepting the quiet intimacy. Her lashes were wet and she didn't know if it was from the sprinkler or if she was crying but when Chad drew back and noticed he used a corner of the towel to dry her eyes, tenderly, like he might for one of his children.

Piper didn't want him to do it. She didn't want to care for him or his family, this wonderful family that worked so well as a team and obviously loved each other completely.

"Why me?" she whispered.

He looked at her helplessly before answering. "Because…" He struggled to find the words. "Because—I just knew." Agitated, he started rubbing her with the towel again. "I felt it. I never expected to feel it a second time."

She needed to understand. "What did you feel?"

He shook his head and smiled and there was warmth in his eyes when he stopped his hands. "The same thing you felt when you saw me."

He remembered that first night, more importantly, he knew she did too. "I want to keep seeing you."

"Chad, I need to tell you something." She put her hand against his chest and stepped back.

Her tone made him nervous. "Tell me then."

Piper wrapped herself protectively in the towel and walked around the counter to take a stool across from him.

"I came here six months ago in order to put some distance

between myself and a bad relationship." She breathed in and out as though even discussing it was somehow exhausting. "I found myself in a caretaker role. I didn't appreciate it. He put every responsibility onto my shoulders and I loathed him for it."

Chad's gaze caressed her sympathetically. "I know, you told me this already."

Piper's lower lip trembled and she looked up apologetically. "Chad, your kids are great. I could never have gotten Mick to help with dinner or clean up or anything else for that matter and he's an adult but right now I just don't think I'm ready to consider getting involved with a man with a family. I'm still carrying too much resentment. I only want to think about myself for a while." She cringed. "I realize that sounds selfish but I've earned a break. It would be wrong of me to give you the wrong impression about why I'm here and worse, to confuse Kenny and Missy about us. I'm sorry."

The corner of Chad's mouth trembled a moment then curled up in amusement. "This isn't a marriage proposal, Piper. I just want to hang out with you more. I don't have much of a social life outside of this." He waved his hand around the kitchen. "We can keep it light, no demands, if that's what you need."

"It is, right now it is."

"Fine, no pressure." He grinned. "You free tomorrow?"

12

Now that school was officially out for the summer Chad was confined to his home office most of the time. Still, there were always situations that demanded on-site calls and he pounced on them. Unfortunately, if Mrs. Conway from next door wasn't home to watch the kids while he ran around he was forced to drag them along. Today was one of those days.

When he pulled onto the dusty gravel and parked, his was the lone car among the pickup trucks and SUVs.

Chad cut the engine. After he unclipped his seatbelt he reached over and slapped Missy's visor back up, giving her a fierce look at the same time. It was obvious she was waiting for him to leave so she could make faces at her brother in the mirror. Kenny was already in an ugly mood in the backseat and nurturing a grudge because he didn't call shotgun fast enough. Chad knew one more poke would send Kenny over the edge of his already questionable control.

Chad got out and peered through his open window at his kids, his voice as stern as he could make it.

"No funny business. You stay in the car with your seatbelts buckled."

He looked at Kenny specifically and said, "No kicking the back of Missy's seat and keep your hands to yourself."

Then he turned to his daughter. "Keep the mirror where it is and don't antagonize your brother."

"Yeah!" Kenny said.

"Hey," Chad pointed his finger at both of them. "Here's the deal, if I come back and hear one complaint from either of you—and I don't even care whose fault it is—we won't be stopping for ice cream cones on the way to Grandma's."

"Ice cream cones?" they asked in unison.

"Only if you two can convince me I can trust you together for ten minutes. Think you can do that?"

They both nodded, perfectly sincere and Chad clapped his hardhat on and strode off to find Hanson, leaving his kids to discuss their flavor preferences.

"You're in a good mood." Joy sidled up to Piper as she used a rubber scraper to clear the cake batter from the mixing bowl.

"Am I?" Piper asked, surprised that it showed.

"You've been wearing a perma-grin all day and humming off key so yeah. What gives? Does it have anything to do with that phone call you got here yesterday?"

Piper set the bowl aside and smiled sheepishly. "Maybe. Let's just say that I have plans this weekend and with summer here my nights are wide open. That's all."

"Wait a second. You're busy? You had a date, didn't you? I knew it!" Joy leaned her hip against the counter and peered at her co-worker expectantly.

Piper shrugged. "I wouldn't call it a date exactly."

"Nuh uh. No way. I need details, Chicky."

Piper tossed the rubber scraper into the bowl and faced her. "It's nothing, it's just, do you remember that guy I was so pissed at a couple of weeks ago?"

"The stalker?"

Piper laughed and shook her head. "He's not a stalker. I was just mad at him but now I'm over it. He's actually a really nice guy."

"And?"

"We sort of got together recently. Not alone," she clarified. "His kids were there, too."

"No!" Then Joy made a face. "He's got kids?"

"Two. Eight-year-old twins."

"That's a lot of baggage."

"Cut it out," Piper warned. "Besides, it's not like we're dating.

We're just hanging out together. I could use another friend. You know I'm not looking for anything else right now."

"So you said." Joy snorted skeptically. "And what's he looking for?"

This is where Piper had to tread delicately. "Well, he might have hoped for more at first but I set him straight. We had a good heart to heart and now he's perfectly content to leave it at that." Piper frowned at the doubt clearly written across Joy's face. "Hey, don't look at me like that. I like him—*them*. We have fun together. Why does there have to be more?"

"I get it. He's not very good looking."

Piper bit her lip to stifle a giggle. "Hardly. The guy's tastier than a black forest cake. But that's beside the point." She took a second to roll her shoulders before sliding the last heavy cake pan into the oven with the others, and when she turned around she was grinning. "I'm taking him windsurfing after work today."

"What about his kids?"

"They'll be with their grandmother."

"Not their mom?"

"I hope not, she's been dead for years."

"Hold it, he's a widower?"

"Yeah, so what?" Piper answered lightly.

Joy stepped in Piper's way and forced her to look at her. "This is a pretty loaded situation you've landed in."

"No way." Piper brushed past her. "Anyway, you told me yourself I should be out there making new friends and now you're warning me off?"

"Okay, tell me something. This is a family we're talking about, right? So what happens when the kids start bonding with you, counting on you, seeing you as a mother figure? Are you going to bail again? Pick up and leave town the minute your independent status is threatened?"

Now Piper was angry. "That's not how it happened last time and you know it. This is nothing like the situation with Mick.

Chad's cool with the ground rules so I'm willing to make a little room on my schedule for him—*them*," she corrected herself, "as long as they respect the boundaries."

It was apparent that Joy didn't believe her, but who the hell cared? Let her make her ridiculous assumptions. Obviously there wasn't anything Piper could say at this point that would convince her but having the last laugh was going to be sweet.

Piper didn't feel a single qualm about meeting Chad alone at his house. She was still skating along on her righteous indignation and it carried her confidently up his driveway, two boards secured to the roof of her car.

When she knocked a disembodied voice yelled, "Come on in. Door's open."

It took a minute for her eyes to adjust from the bright sunshine outside and the dim interior of the foyer.

"Where are you?" she called.

"Upstairs, be right down."

Piper sat on the steps and leaned back against the wall, pulling her knees up and stretching her long t-shirt over them. How long did it take a guy to dress, anyway?

She looked up when Chad's bedroom door opened and he came around the corner tying his swim trunks. The sight of him tilted her world on end. He looked so unbelievably appealing that she jumped up and backed away, anxious to get out of the house before she did or said something stupid and irreversible.

He gave her an easy smile as he started down the stairs. "I see you're all set."

She needed to chill, fast, and to do that she couldn't look at his face. Her eyes raced desperately down his body but it only got worse.

How the hell could he come off so cool and relaxed when she was nearly swooning at the sight of his furry muscular legs? It wasn't fair. His chest, his arms, even his abs, sure, she expected those to shake a woman up, but his *legs*? What was wrong with her? She tried to calculate where she was in her cycle but her brain was misfiring. Piper dropped her eyes one more time to his feet, the one thing guaranteed not to drive her out of her senses. Ah crap. She let out a big mental groan because even his bare feet were turning her on. *He's a friend*, she insisted. *Just a friend.*

"You'll want a shirt," she said weakly. *Please, I'm begging you here. Put on a shirt.* She didn't like how her eyes moved up to that wonderful chest of his and lingered.

"I left it in the kitchen. I was hoping you'd put a little sunscreen on my back first. I can do yours too if you like. I have plenty."

Piper followed him back, her brain weighing the risks of allowing him to rub lotion on her versus declining the offer and letting her fair and freckled shoulders bear the consequences. In the end she agreed to the lotion.

Chad snatched the bottle off the counter and slapped it into her hand.

Piper read the label and laughed. "SPF forty-five?"

"Hey, it's what I have around for the kids."

Then Chad did something so unexpectedly playful that it completely disarmed her. He turned and put both hands on the top of the counter and spread his legs like a man about to be frisked.

"Where did I leave my handcuffs?" Piper asked with a smirk.

He turned and shot her a wicked grin but the lighthearted banter died an uneasy death as soon as she stepped between his feet and began smoothing the lotion over his warm skin. The toughest moment by far was when she had to run her hands along the edge of his waistband. She kept her head but just barely. It was a relief to step away and give his back one final slap.

"There, you're all set."

Chad straightened up and grabbed the bottle off the counter. He walked over to one of the stools and took a seat.

"Come here." He patted his thigh.

"Shouldn't I hear a please?"

He made a face at her and Piper was reminded of Kenny.

"With sugar on top," he added daringly.

"No funny business," she warned him, walking over.

Chad held up his hands innocently. "Promise."

Piper presented her back and Chad spread his knees and tugged her between them. She was suddenly alive to the tickle of his coarse legs brushing all along her bare thighs and calves. It was so unsettling that she nearly jumped when he started rolling her shirt up to expose her back. One smooth tug and Chad released the bottom knot of her bikini and her breasts along with it. Startled, Piper clapped her hands over both, stubbornly pressing the spandex back where it belonged.

"Hey!" She shot Chad a sharp look over her shoulder. "You didn't have to untie that."

"Shh," he gentled her. "This makes it easier but I'll leave the top knot tied if you prefer."

"I prefer."

Chad chuckled and the next thing she knew, his warm hands were flowing over her shoulders and flaring up her neck on both sides, just coming to a stop before her hair. He wrapped his legs around her thighs to keep her close as he kneaded her muscles and worked the lotion over her at the same time.

To her surprise and silent gratitude he was actually giving her a massage—and she wasn't about to complain. It was much too long since she enjoyed something so heavenly.

Chad took a second squirt, then started at the small of her back and ran his thumbs along her spine as his fingers fanned out, long enough to curl over her sides.

Piper moaned and Chad's smile deepened. He was glad the massage was working for both of them.

"There," she directed him to a painful knot under her shoulder blade. His hand flowed back to it and while he worked it out with unrelenting pressure Piper's eyes fell closed and her head lolled forward.

He rubbed patiently at the knot until it was only a faint memory. Piper drooped, completely relaxed as the last of her accumulated tension eased. That is until she felt Chad's hands run along her sides one last time and his fingertips lightly graze along the sides of her breasts.

Piper leaped away and her voice wasn't remotely steady when she said, "Good, I guess we should get going then."

Chad found her blush unbelievably attractive but he nodded, perfectly aware he just unintentionally ruined the moment. "I'll be right with you."

It was a dismissal that Piper took swift advantage of, hurrying out to secure her top in private.

Only when Piper was gone did Chad willingly stand. He looked down his body with a sharp snort and wondered how he was supposed to lower the main sail. Never had he fully appreciated the tenting quality of swim trunks like he did now. Piper was skittish enough without adding the enjoyable rub down session to the mix. Imagine how freaked she'd be if she saw the condition she'd left him in.

Chad slipped into his t-shirt then picked up the crossword puzzle and pen still sitting on the counter from that morning, hoping a few clues would be enough to distract him until he toned it down a bit.

Only when he felt it was safe to rejoin Piper did Chad toss the paper aside and grab his keys and sunglasses off the microwave.

13

Piper pulled her key out of the ignition and turned on Chad. "I'm not a bad driver."

"I never said you were." He opened the passenger door and climbed out.

She hopped out on her side and scowled over the hood at him. "You implied it," she said, moving to release her board from the roof.

"I said nothing of the kind. What I said was that I feel more comfortable in the driver's seat. That's all. Stop acting all defensive. It had nothing to do with you or your skill as a driver."

"So it's a guy thing."

Chad craned his head to see her over the roof. "Probably. Now, will you show me how to get my board free?"

He thought it was funny that she parked in the exact same spot he took that afternoon just over two weeks ago when he spotted her car. Considering the incident had the stink of voyeurism clinging to it Chad opted to keep that little detail to himself.

They slipped into their lifejackets then picked up their boards, carrying them into the choppy waves. The wind was with them today.

Chad took a second to wet himself down and adjust to the cool water.

Since he already had experience on snowboards and water skis, things she'd never tried herself, Piper expected today's lesson to go smoother for Chad than her first time out.

"You have to climb onto the board and it isn't dignified. No one can do this gracefully so don't even bother. If you don't adjust to the feel of the board right away, just keep trying. It took me more attempts than I care to remember just to master standing."

"Why don't you show me?"

"No comments and no sniggering. I mean it," she warned.

Piper kneeled on the rocking board then worked carefully to her feet, keeping her knees slightly bent for stability while she hauled the sail up with the cord until she could grab the boom.

"Looks simple enough," Chad said.

Piper eased her mast back down then leaped back, away from the board to spot him if necessary.

His first attempt to get up from his knees kicked the board right at her when he fell backwards.

"You needed to cool off anyway," she said, teasing him when he came up dripping.

He gave her a long silent look. *Honey, you don't know the half of it.*

But he was determined to do this so he paid attention to her directions and was on his feet on his second attempt.

Piper was astonished. Sure, she knew he'd get up eventually, but this fast? Rather than give in to envy she chose to take his success as a compliment to herself. After all, who showed him how to do it in the first place? Piper cheered as he started hauling up the mast.

"Wait," she began, "You're ... " "Losing it" was what she didn't get a chance to say.

Chad did a couple of Elvis Presley hip jerks and dropped the cord as he tumbled backwards again.

Piper was laughing when he broke out of the water. "Nice pelvic thrusts there, rock star!"

He wiped the water from his face. "Hey, I thought we weren't going to ridicule each other."

"Oh, that only goes for us professionals. You're fresh meat. It's essential that you get a healthy sense of your limitations."

"Nice," he said sarcastically, slapping a handful of water at her. She ducked out of the way and came up expecting a second spray of water but he reached across the board and caught her wrist instead.

"Listen, I won't splash you if you can manage to keep your criticisms to yourself."

"Or what?" she taunted. "You'll gather up your Matchbox Cars and go home? I brought you here."

"I remember the crazy driving."

"Ha ha," she said with a sneer. "Try again, Elvis."

"Elvis?" He shook his head. "No, don't explain, I can guess."

He didn't need her help this time and before she could even clamor onto her own board he was setting off across the water without her.

Piper drew her sail up, turned her head, and saw him wobbling. She yelled out, "Think of the number seven!"

What? Chad turned and looked back, an anxious look on his face.

"Make your body a number seven!" she repeated.

He caught it this time and adjusted. Damn, he was good. Better than she ever was, even after months of practice.

They made a run along the shoreline, a safe distance from the docks and buoys but close enough to land in case he ran into trouble. He didn't.

It was impossible not to make comparisons between Chad and Mick as she pursued him. The difference in style was obvious. Mick was a daredevil, a wild child, unafraid to hit the wakes of boats and go airborne. He flirted with disaster and with every wipeout he came up cheering.

Chad, on the other hand, had competence seeping out of his pores. Watching his easy mastery of the sail, no one would guess it was his first time out. He was a natural athlete, the board an extension of his body and he handled it that way.

At first Piper watched over Chad out of concern but as it became apparent that she had nothing to worry about her manner of watching him shifted entirely. She became all too aware of how his wet trunks clung, showing off solid muscle and bulges she had no business noticing. His hair was already partially dry and it fluttered in the wind, catching the sun.

"It's just hair," she muttered.

Then he turned and flashed a gorgeous smile and Piper's heart did a somersault.

All told, Chad wiped out three times, twice while he was trying to execute a turn to head back. There was a point where he started running out into deeper water but Piper was able to coach him back. When they cut into shore where they started she was insanely proud of him. He was awesome.

Piper turned away while Chad slipped out of his life vest and stepped onto the grass to squeeze the excess water out of his shorts. Friends didn't look at each other like that, she reminded herself. She'd already stolen more peeks than she could count and that sort of nonsense had to stop.

Refocused, she was all business again, maybe even a little brusque while they secured their boards to the top of her car but he didn't seem to notice. While he spread extra towels over their seats Piper ran around behind the car to slip into her big t-shirt again. Although it was merely cotton, it still managed to serve very nicely as body armor because it restored a sense of security to Piper that she hadn't felt in hours.

Chad turned his dark glasses on Piper when she got behind the wheel. "Dinner's on me."

"No. I owe you a meal this time."

"Consider it your fee—payment for the lesson. I really enjoyed this."

Piper smiled. "All right, that sounds reasonable."

Since they weren't exactly dressed for a restaurant, dining options were limited to drive-thru. Chad suggested a seafood place on the way to his house and Piper agreed.

When they got to the house, Chad offered Piper the use of the kid's shower. They split up and went their separate ways, putting dinner off for the moment. Afterwards, clean and refreshed, Piper went looking for Chad and found him in the kitchen taking plates from the cabinet.

"Can I get a plastic bag for my wet things?" she asked.

"Here." He held out his hand. "I'll hang them outside with mine."

She waited just inside the screen door while he decorated his railing with more wet clothing.

"You need a clothesline," she said as he came back inside.

Chad laughed. "There's a thought."

They ate Japanese style at the coffee table. The mood was surprisingly relaxed as they laughed and chatted while picking at the food between them. Piper chalked it up to being fully dressed. She never even noticed she wasn't uncomfortable eating in front of him now.

She really liked Chad but she knew she had to keep her head straight. Keeping things light was critical if they were going to have any chance at being friends. He was good company, fun to be around. She couldn't allow herself to be seduced by his beautiful packaging.

Piper shifted on her knees and grabbed a fresh napkin.

"Hey," she said, looking around. "You know, I just realized something. You don't have a dining room."

Chad took a hush puppy. "Technically we do but I converted it into my office."

"You work at home?"

"As much as I can."

She grimaced. "I can't believe I haven't asked this yet but what do you do exactly?"

He laughed. "Exactly? I'm a contractor."

Piper nodded. "I can picture that." She rose up on her knees and playfully waved a popcorn shrimp in front of him. "Last chance, only one left."

What was she doing? Talk about blundering into a charged situation. Piper froze, her hand suspended in mid-air as she stared at Chad with wide eyes. Before she could pull back he caught her wrist and brought the shrimp to his mouth. Neither of them blinked as he ate it right out from between her fingers. The faint brush of his lips set off a seismic tremor inside Piper.

Then Chad swallowed and with a deft turn of his hand, drew her fingertips into his mouth. The heat, the sensation of his tongue swirling around her fingers, licking them clean was exquisite torture. It was a wonder her chest managed to contain a heart so bent on blowing her ribcage wide open.

Piper's anxiety was genuine when she pulled her hand back.

"What are you doing?" she asked, visibly shaken and flushed.

"Too subtle?" His husky reply was both seductive and deeply stirring. She was in serious trouble.

"Don't." She rose up and started picking up their trash, frantically stuffing everything into the take-out bags.

"Piper." He spoke softly, barely a whisper yet it stilled her shaking hands.

The last thing she wanted to do at that moment was look at him, knowing how he pulled at her, but she couldn't help it.

He gave her a long, penetrating look. "Do you honestly believe you don't want me?"

Why did he have to ask that? For an instant she could have sworn she saw a flash of vulnerability in his eyes, an echo of her own. Then it was gone.

Piper was never comfortable lying so she chose to be evasive instead. "Whether I do or I don't isn't the issue. I don't want to complicate things between us."

Chad pressed on. "Why?"

She scowled and picked up another napkin. "You know why. I've already told you that I don't want to get serious about anyone right now. You're a gor—" The word *gorgeous* almost slipped out.

"Good-looking man. There must be a lot of women who would kill to have you pursue them."

"What if I'd rather chase you?"

Piper expelled a deep, exasperated breath. "Chad, I like you. I really like you and the last thing I want to do is hurt you or your kids. Can't you see that? I'm not ready for more and I can't say when I will be." She threw back her head and squeezed her eyes shut tight. "Maybe I'm expecting too much from you. You're in a different place than I am and it isn't fair to you. I should probably just go. This was a mistake."

They stood up at the same time.

"Don't," he said, laying his hand on her arm for one brief moment.

"Don't what?"

"Don't go. You're right, you did clarify everything for me and I owe you an apology for getting carried away tonight." He attempted to reassure her with a smile. "Blame it on seeing you in a bathing suit again and then coming back here to an empty house."

"Are you serious?" she asked doubtfully.

"I'm not a saint, Piper, and I haven't had sex in … too long. My gonads got the better of me. I won't let it happen again. Friends?"

"You can handle it?"

"Absolutely."

"I'll hold you to it."

He grinned and held out his hand. "I know you will."

14

It was over his morning coffee that Chad had a flash of inspiration. Okay, sure, no question he screwed up last night by turning up the heat under Piper's sweet derriere so soon. He needed to back off and trust her that she wasn't ready to get involved yet but by god she was wavering, like a mighty pine about to come down.

It didn't take a genius to recognize there was no way she was going to pop over again without either a compelling reason or a guarantee that they wouldn't be alone together. He needed to lure her back and reassure her that he wasn't a threat. He wanted her to feel comfortable around him again so a wary distance wasn't an option.

Whether he wanted to be or not he was in a battle of wills with Piper. She was working damned hard to convince herself that she didn't want him but the outcome was weighted heavily in his favor. It wasn't exactly a fair fight. She was losing without much effort on his part but the least he could do was resist the urge to push her into a defensive retreat.

So for now he'd focus on being her friend, hopefully an indispensable one. It was time for a new plan.

He had to talk to his mother first.

"Why are you calling so early, is something wrong?" she asked.

"No, something's right. I have a favor, a big one actually."

There was exasperation in her voice. "Let's hear it."

"I was hoping I could persuade you to take your grandchildren one more night."

"Why?"

"I have plans with Piper."

"Really?" She sounded hopeful.

"Almost."

"Call me when it's confirmed."

"I can't, it's sort of a sneak attack."

She groaned. "Chad honey, what are you doing?"

"I screwed up last night and now she's running scared again but I hit on an idea that will fix everything. I hope."

"It sounds like you're about to foul it up even more."

"Trust me."

"Maybe you should just try the truth this time. You know, tell her you care about her and want to take it to the next level."

"Can't—she's not ready to hear that. It'll just scare her off."

"Your father didn't have to work nearly this hard to win me. I don't know what you're doing wrong."

"Mom, did you really want me to know that?"

"What did I say?"

"Never mind." He chuckled. "Listen, I'll talk to you tomorrow, tell you how it went."

"I'll be waiting with bated breath."

When he ended that call Chad scrolled through his contacts until he found the next one.

"Chad?" his friend answered. "What's going on?"

"Brent, do you and Pam have anything planned for tonight?"

"Not a thing. Why?"

"I owe you a dinner. Can you come over?"

"Let me put Pam on."

When Chad hung up his smile was so wide his cheeks tingled. Zippering his fingers together he reached up for a long luxuriant stretch before clasping his hands behind his head and kicking back in his chair with a satisfied sigh.

Joy slid a tray of frosted cookies into the display case and pulled the door closed. Looking up she saw that Piper was bent over yet another special order cake with a scowl of concentration on her face.

"Are you about ready for a coffee break?" Joy asked.

"Yes," Piper said, clearly exhausted. "I've just got this little bit left on this one then I really need to shake out my wrist."

"You're not getting carpal are you?"

"Not yet but I'm being careful."

Joy drifted over and watched her finish. She nodded slowly. "Nice."

"Thanks."

"Come on, I already put the *Back in Ten* sign on the case."

Piper stretched up, straightening her stiff back. The yawn came out of nowhere and Joy laughed at her.

"Still not used to it yet," Joy said. "Don't worry, it'll come"

While Joy poured two cups of coffee Piper shook out her hand then bent it back at the wrist, holding that position for a minute.

Joy walked over and handed her a cup and they walked around the corner and out of view, pulling out their stools.

"So, you've been pretty mum about yesterday, how'd it go?" Joy asked, eyeing Piper over the rim of her cup.

Piper shrugged uncertainly. "It started out okay but then Chad had to go and ruin it by making a pass at me."

Joy's eyes widened in mock horror. "The bastard!"

Piper giggled. "Cut it out."

"So ... now what?"

Piper shrugged helplessly. "I wish I knew. He says he can handle the friendship thing but I have my doubts." She buried her fingers into her hair and tugged. "The thing is, I like him. If I'd met him say, six months, maybe even a year from now, I'd definitely be interested, but the timing's off."

"And?"

"And nothing. I think I have to back up. I don't want to lead him on." She frowned at Joy. "Tell me something. Am I right in assuming that he's exactly the kind of guy most women are looking for?"

"Which is?"

"A successful homeowner with a great personality and an even better body." Piper took a sip of coffee and held up her finger as she swallowed. "Not to mention a killer smile and lips that know exactly what they're doing."

Joy sat up taller. "Hold it. I think you skipped something there and that tasty detail should have come out first. He kissed you?"

Piper squirmed uncomfortably. "Yes."

"Is this what you call *not* dating?"

Piper rolled her eyes. "That was a one time deal—okay two, but they happened in succession and we sorted it out. Or I thought we did until last night."

Joy shook her head, bemused. "I don't know what to think about this double life you're leading."

"Can we get back to my question please?"

"I forgot it."

Piper laughed. "Aren't most women looking to hook a guy like this?"

"Absolutely."

"So why does he seem to be set on me?"

"I don't know. You're such a prickly bitch," Joy said with a playful grin.

"Thank you," Piper said sarcastically.

"Oh sorry, I thought I was helping," Joy teased. She tapped her cheekbone with her finger a few times. "Maybe he's one of those guys that like the chase."

"I don't think so. Guys like that don't typically settle down and go all dependable."

"Now he's dependable too? What a loser. You really need to kick his ass back to his own freaky dimension."

Piper grumbled up at the ceiling. "Why do I even bother

talking to you?"

"Besides not knowing too many people around here? Easy, that's what best friends do." Joy slid off her stool. "Break's over."

Chad closed the oven and gave a little cheer. He wiped his hands on the towel tucked into the waistband of his jeans, picking up the song he'd been humming where he left off. So far, so bad. Everything was beautiful baby.

Piper was just walking into her apartment when her cell phone rang. She went digging frantically through her purse as she kicked the door closed behind her.

"Hello?"

"Piper? What a relief. I'm so glad I caught you. Listen, I'm having a bit of a crisis and I could really use your help. Could you come over?"

"Chad, I'm not sure that's such a good idea." Piper toed off her shoes and made her way to the bedroom to get a clean change of clothes for after her shower.

"This has nothing to do with yesterday, I swear. I wouldn't have called if I didn't honestly need your help."

"What kind of help?"

"You know those friends I blew off a few weeks ago?"

"Yeah," she said slowly.

"I was going to make it up to them by having them over for dinner tonight but it's a disaster. I don't know if I can save my roast. Would you come and look at it? Please?"

"You made a roast?"

"I'll let you answer that when you see it. It doesn't resemble anything I've ever eaten before."

"If that's the case what else have you got lying around?"

"Corn dogs in the freezer and mac and cheese."

"Run to the store right now and pick up some nice steaks, I'll hit the market by my place and be right over with whatever else I can find. What time are they coming?"

"They'll be here in an hour."

"Do you have any wine?"

"Of course."

"Good, it'll relax them and give us time to pull everything together."

"Thanks, Piper."

"I'll be there as soon as I can."

He hung up and broke into a happy whistle.

Chad barely got the front door open before Piper brushed right past him and headed directly for the kitchen carrying a bulging canvas bag.

"Do you want to see the roast?" he asked, following her down the hall.

"Why not?" She set the bag on the counter and started unpacking spring onions, fresh asparagus, peppers, and baby red potatoes. She was particularly careful with the grape tomatoes and lettuce.

Chad stared at the produce spilling across his counter with his mouth hanging open. "What'd you do, buy them out?"

"You owe me thirty-two dollars."

"No problem."

She flattened the bag and turned. "Okay, let's see it."

He bent and pulled out the oven rack then folded back the foil.

Piper drew back, hiding her smile behind her hand. "Are your smoke detectors working properly?"

"Ha ha."

"How'd you do that?"

He replaced the foil and shoved it back in. "I don't know."

"Well don't leave it in there. That needs to be dumped."

"You can't save it?"

"Maybe two hours ago."

"So I cooked it too long?"

"I doubt that's all that went wrong here today but at least we're on the right track now. Why don't you throw a pot on the stove for the potatoes while I wash the lettuce?"

"Then what should I do?"

"Go light the grill and after you're done out there, I'll have something else for you to do. This is your party not mine."

When Chad's guests arrived the steaks were just about to go on the grill, the potatoes were nearly done, the salad looked beautiful, and the bottle of red wine was uncorked and breathing.

Piper hid out in the kitchen when Chad went to greet them. He ushered them into the living room then went back for Piper.

Dragging her through the archway Chad announced, "Tonight's dinner might not have happened if not for the cool intervention of this woman here. Piper Frost, take a bow."

He stepped back and beamed at her. Piper rolled her eyes at him then looked at the bewildered couple. "He ruined his roast."

"We're having roast?" said Pam.

"Not anymore. Now it's steak," said Chad.

"Now it's edible," Piper amended with a laugh.

"Piper, meet my two oldest friends."

"Oldest?" Pam said with a shudder.

Chad laughed. "Okay my *closest* friends—Brent and Pam Fuller."

"Hello," Piper said, a tad bashfully.

"Hi," the Fullers replied in unison and everyone laughed again.

Chad leaned in. "Anyone interested in a glass of wine?"

"If you're pouring I won't say no," said Pam.

"Brent?"

"Sure. I'll give you a hand."

Chad walked out, plunking the unofficial hostess duties squarely on Piper's shoulders.

"Why don't we sit down?" she said, motioning towards the sofa.

"Good idea."

They settled onto the cushions and looked at each other awkwardly, nodding and smiling for a moment. Piper broke the ice with a question. "So how long have you known Chad?"

Pam's brows pinched together as she did the mental calculation. "Hmm, I'd say it's been what, twelve years now."

Piper smiled. "So you can vouch for him then?"

"I've done it before," Pam said with a twinkle in her eye, "when I introduced him to my best friend, Chelsea."

Piper cringed. "Oh my god, I just walked right into that one. I'm so sorry."

Pam smiled, shaking her head. "Don't be. It's not a decision I regret. Not a bit. Chad made her happy."

"You must miss her."

"We all do, but it gets easier every year." Pam's expression softened and she smiled at Piper. "I'm so glad Chad's finally going out again. You have no idea how much I worried about him."

"Oh, we're not dating," Piper said hastily, correcting her mistake. "It isn't like that between us. We're just friends."

Taken aback for a moment, Pam didn't get an opportunity to pursue it because the men returned. Brent strolled over to his wife and handed her a glass then settled into the nearest wing chair.

"Guess this one's for you," Chad said handing his second glass to Piper before claiming the remaining chair.

"Hold it," Brent said before anyone took a sip. "I want to make a toast."

Pam stared hard at her husband, trying to communicate something to him while Chad shot him a warning look of his own across the coffee table. Brent just winked back and sat forward, holding out his glass, "Here's to round two."

Chad's eyes bulged in alarm. The idiot was going to ruin everything.

Grinning at his friend's panic Brent said simply, "Let's call it flank steak."

Flank steak my ass, Chad thought as he leaned in to rap his glass against the others. Luckily Piper didn't read anything more into it but if he didn't haul Brent to the side soon and explain a few things to him all his best-laid plans were going to come crashing down on his head.

They had their little chat outside by the grill while Piper and Pam sat at the kitchen table drawing fresh vegetables through dip and chatting like old friends.

Chad leaned back to peer around Brent and spy on them through the screen door. Piper was laughing and nudging Pam's arm at what she was hearing. He could tell by body language alone when Pam said, "I swear."

That probably wasn't good. What was she telling Piper, anyway?

"Chad?" Brent said slowly. "Are you going to turn the steak or do you want me to do it?"

"Huh?"

Brent laughed. "Man—you are gone."

"Don't say that."

"Just stating the obvious."

"If Piper hears that she's out of here."

Brent twisted open a beer. The wine was fine as an appetizer but he needed sustenance.

"I don't get it. She likes you—even I can see that, and I'm not the most perceptive guy in the world."

"Yeah." Chad flipped the steak then closed the lid. "That old boyfriend of hers sure did a number on her. I'd love to track him down and punch him right in the face."

Brent's eyebrows went up at the simmering anger in his friend. "What did he do to her?"

"Used her, drained her, and then threw her away."

"Prick."

"Big time."

"So he's casting a shadow over your love life."

"Looks that way. Let me have some of that." Chad held out his hand and Brent passed him the beer. Chad took a good swallow then handed it back.

"Can I say something?" Brent asked cautiously.

"Maybe."

"You need to pull it back a notch."

Chad chuckled at himself, at the situation, at the whole bloody mess of it. "How am I supposed to do that?"

"You can't take your eyes off of Piper and it shows. The way you feel about her is in your eyes, blatantly, man, that's all. You should know that if you think you're going to pull this off."

Chad groaned. "Oh hell."

15

Chad's best friends did him a huge favor that night by being more spirited, more amusing than ever. Their stories and anecdotes were so entertaining that they managed to keep both Chad and Piper distracted from each other.

At the end of the night Pam and Piper exchanged telephone numbers and then Brent took hold of his wife's arm and towed her out to their car. Chad and Piper waved them off from the door then returned to the kitchen to do the clean up.

"You don't have to stick around and help with this," Chad told her, taking a wine glass out of her hand. "You've done plenty already."

"That's okay. I don't mind." When she saw him putting the stemware into the upper basket of the dishwasher she intervened. "These should be washed by hand. They could get broken in there."

"If they break I'll replace them. They're not expensive."

"Chad," she said wearily. "It's the principle of the thing." She put them in the sink. "I'll wash them myself. Just leave them."

"You and my mother would get along great," he said with amusement.

Piper went out to the living room, bringing the other two glasses back with her. "I liked your friends. They're really nice." She started running water into the sink.

Chad looked up from his work. "Thanks. I suppose they'll do."

She watched the dish soap foam up. "Pam said she introduced you to Chelsea."

He set another plate in the dishwasher. "She did. They were best friends from way back. When Pam started dating Brent— "

"Your roommate."

"Right, they maneuvered Chelsea and me into a double date. As soon as we saw each other that was it. We were a foursome, then two distinct but close pairs. They're Missy and Kenny's godparents."

"No kidding."

"Yep." He stood the silverware in the baskets.

"Would you mind if I called Pam?"

He looked up. "Why would I?"

"I don't know. I just wanted to be sure it wouldn't hurt you."

He smiled, touched. "Call her."

Piper sat at the counter and watched Chad wipe everything down. She liked that he was neat. "Can I ask you something personal?"

He didn't stop but the sponge moved slower as he scrubbed at a spot on the top of the stove. "Go ahead."

"What do you miss most about your wife?"

He turned. "Chelsea," he said carefully, walking the sponge back to the sink. "I don't think I can break her down like that. Sometimes it's the way she smelled or the sound of her voice. Coming home to a house with her in it and simply knowing everything was right." He sighed. "I miss her company. It was nice having someone who, even when she didn't agree with me, understood where I'm coming from. Seeing her every day never stopped feeling good. Like hot tea for a sore throat and spontaneous laughter all rolled into one."

"Wow," Piper whispered.

"Do you know that feeling of contentment, that utter happiness you can get just coming home after a long day or after being out of town? It's like a full-body sigh of relief."

"Like coming home from camp," she murmured.

He nodded. "You do understand. You feel like life makes sense again, you're back to normal. That's how it felt every single day."

And he'd lost that. Piper was choking up inside just picturing this gaping hole in his chest.

Chad grimaced. "I hate how this sounds but I miss the sex, too.

It was hard not being able to reach for her at night, curl around her."

"Why should admitting that bother you? You were in your prime when you lost her. It's perfectly understandable."

He laughed. "Is my prime already over?"

She smiled. "No, of course not but you know what I mean."

"Yeah, I do."

A sad little smile flared across his face then winked out. "We wanted each other all the time. We could have ignored eating if the kids weren't there to ground us in reality. As much as we loved Kenny and Missy they were an extension of our feelings for each other not the heart of our marriage. Our relationship was the nucleus of the family."

Touched, Piper said kindly, "I think that's a good thing. How many marriages collapse because the commitment between the parents is shunted aside when kids enter the picture? I know a few. Any kid would be lucky to grow up in a family where the parents are in love and committed to each other. Who wouldn't want that kind of marriage for themselves? A loving marriage is the best example you can give a kid."

"That's what we thought, hoped anyway."

She smiled. "Someday when I grow up, maybe I'll be lucky enough to find that."

"From what I can tell you're already grown up."

"I know, but I'm intentionally reverting."

"*Can* you intentionally revert? Doesn't it take a head injury or something?"

"Why leave everything to chance?" She kicked the bottom of her stool a couple of times, weighing something. Finally she gave in. "Do you think you'll ever find that again? What you had with Chelsea?"

He leaned back against the counter and tipped his head to the side. "For years I doubted it, now I realize that was the grief talking. I'm pretty confident."

He put some soap in the dishwasher and started it up. Piper

was watching him silently when he turned with her canvas bag in his hands.

"I'm not sure if I have exact change but I can give you what I have and owe you the rest," he said as he handed her the bag.

"Whenever."

"I know where to find you, anyway."

She laughed. "That's true."

"I'll walk you out." He took her arm and turned her down the hall.

Tenderness for this man was blooming to life inside her and he was walking her to the door? Tonight he had to behave like a perfect gentleman? Piper didn't know what to think. She was all screwed up, all confused.

Just as Chad reached out to take the doorknob Piper turned and leaned heavily against the door, keeping it closed. She took a deep steadying breath.

"I'd be lying if I said I wasn't attracted to you or that I haven't fantasized about, well, getting intimate, but what happens then? I don't have many friends here and I worry about ruining the friendship that we're building between us if I give in to those temptations. I'd rather keep the friendship if I have to make a choice."

His surprise was obvious. "Who says there has to be a choice? Friendships are the best basis for deeper relationships."

She smiled weakly. "I knew if I brought this up you'd have a good response but right now that's all I'm prepared to give."

She reached up and stroked the side of his face. It was a mistake. The look in his eyes was killer. There was so much roiling around in them, a storm of emotions he held inside that were suddenly spilling out across his face as he looked at her, needed her. It was unnerving to see how much he was hauling back by the reins. The effort it took had to be incredible.

There was an ache inside her too, as though she was letting them both down but she wanted to believe she was doing the right thing, leaving before regrets could start and the irreversible happened.

Please don't stop me, please don't stop me. Those words repeated over and over in her head. She knew, was absolutely certain that one more word, one more look from him would destroy her already shaky determination to leave.

"Thanks for coming over and helping me tonight. You were awesome," he said.

She was still leaning against the door but she didn't know why. No, that wasn't true, she knew why, wasn't comfortable exploring it, felt compelled to remain anyway. This just sucked.

"Have you ever heard of friends with benefits?" Piper asked then launched herself into Chad's arms.

16

To say that Chad was staggered was putting it mildly. Just when he least expected it, Piper gave in—to the lust, the curiosity, to every damned thing she fought not to trifle with.

She combed her fingernails through his hair then grabbed a hard handful and hauled him down for a hungry kiss. He didn't need a translator to understand what she wanted when she ran her tongue over his lips. He opened to her and wolfed her down, his arms tugging her powerfully against him.

Chad let her take him where she would but not without pangs of doubt. Should he step back, set her away from him and ask whether she really wanted to do this or did he simply let her take control? Of course, offering her an out was the last thing he wanted to do. Then he thought, screw it. If she was willing to revise her own rules why fight it? Her plan beat the pants off of his.

Piper's surrender to the attraction sizzling between them was indisputable, a physical thing. Once committed, the confident decisive woman who warned Chad off with mace was back. He liked this sexy side of her.

Chad broke the kiss to draw a ragged breath then veered right and grazed his rough cheek along her jaw, down her neck, then finally nuzzled her ear. The sensations set Piper vibrating in his arms but it was the tip of his tongue tracing along the shell of her ear that prompted her desperate groan. Piper skimmed her hands down his chest and reached around his waist. Without warning she clapped them firmly on his ass.

Taken by surprise Chad rose a good four inches before settling back on his heels, slightly dazed. Oh no, this was not the same woman who held him off for three excruciating weeks. For some inexplicable reason Piper was making a complete about face and lowering her barricades. Chad wasn't complaining.

Only someone who's endured a self-imposed diet for one too many days only to find themselves suddenly confronted by a buffet table set with all of their favorites could understand this kind of surrender. Piper was overwhelmed by the compulsion to feast, the need to gorge on what she denied herself.

To hell with being seduced. If she was going to cave in to her needs, she was going to be an active player. There was nothing ambiguous about the way her lips moved over Chad, tasting and licking, sucking his chin, his lobe. He let her mood and the momentum she set carry him along on the current. Her hands returned to his chest and she clutched his shirt then proceeded to devour every bare inch of skin she could reach.

"Are you always this aggressive?" he asked, the words followed by yet another deep moan. Chad pulled her head back and went for her throat while one of his hands slipped up under the front of her shirt.

"No." She laughed and gasped, breathless and impatient. "Oh god, kiss me again, please!"

With one hand on the back of her head, the other cupping her breast, Chad obliged. They parried and twirled, thrust and stroked until Piper trembled. If Chad thought by her response that he finally wrested the advantage away from her he was mistaken. Piper easily took it back again by sliding her hand down his body and pressing his straining fly. His eyebrows shot up in surprise.

He drew a shaky breath and caught her wrist. "Careful."

She ignored the warning. "But I need to know."

She shook off his hand then popped the button on his jeans. Chad sighed with relief as the constricting zipper eased down. What happened next was downright embarrassing. His swollen cock sprang through his open fly like a novelty snake shooting out of a can of peanuts.

Piper laughed in delight. "Quick out of the gate, aren't you?"

Without another word she whisked his pants down his legs and Chad kicked them aside. Piper wrapped her hand around the silky yet solid party crasher jutting out of his boxers and purred with approval.

"You're torturing me," Chad groaned against her temple yet he wasn't stopping her.

For the first time in her life Piper was the aggressor and she loved it. Her eyes were glowing as she stroked him, recognizing that what she held in the palm of her hand was prime cut, a filet mignon, reserved specifically for those with a discerning palate. Piper was a gourmand.

She watched Chad sway; his eyes closed tight, his breathing irregular. He wasn't exactly putty in her hand (who'd want that anyway) but close enough. Piper wondered how much farther she could push him. She savored the control but it was time to find Chad's line and test it. There was a wicked smile on her face when she plunged her left hand down the back of his shorts and ripped another gasp right out of him by running her polished nails along his fuzzy crack.

That did it. Chad thought it was pretty safe to assume that since she was the one to break the no contact rule—annihilated it to be more precise—all rules were suspended and he was free to use everything in his arsenal.

Chad eased Piper's hands out of his underwear then caught the bottom of her shirt and, ripping it up and over her head, sent it flying without caring where it landed. Her bra swiftly followed.

Chad took a moment to simply look at Piper's body, bare and beautiful in front of him. His nightly torturous fantasies were over. From here on in, she would know him, his flavor, his texture, his possession, and he would know her. He was going to taste everything. He needed to explore her, divide and conquer her, and Piper was going to thank him for it. Yes, she started this but he was going to finish it.

Chad's eyes locked on Piper's and what she saw in them was a little frightening. She'd poked the caged beast with a stick then set it free. There was an untamed animal hunger flashing in his eyes that she never expected to see. It was thrilling, exhilarating even, to know that he was about to make a meal of her.

Chad swooped down and consumed the air right out of her. She gasped and he thrust his tongue into her mouth, foreshadowing the sexual act to come. Piper swayed dizzily and the hand she'd used to tease and stroke him mere seconds ago now groped for support instead, his erection turned into a railing.

He eased back ever so slowly, the suction of their kiss drawing her lips out until finally the connection broke and Piper's lips sprang back, swollen and sensitive. She drew a ragged breath and stared at him. There was a message in Chad's eyes and it was unmistakable—foreplay was over.

With a move so sudden it made Piper gasp, Chad lifted her off her feet, ripping her hand out of his shorts at the same time. The waistband snapped him hard across the stomach but he didn't flinch. She wasn't even sure he noticed. There was a serious set to his face when he carried her over to the carpeted staircase and set her down.

Piper tugged his boxers down while Chad fought with her slacks. She managed to get a quick arousing glimpse between Chad's legs just before he crawled over her like a panther, caging her between his arms and following her down as she dropped back on the treads. All appetite, he took her mouth and pressed his body full against hers. Her momentary taste of power was over.

Piper's prophetic dream came back to her in sharp detail but it didn't disgust her now. She understood herself for the very first time and wasn't ashamed to want a man. Nothing was more natural. When Chad ran his hands over her, ground his pelvis against her suggestively she rose up to meet him, consumed by the need to join her body with his.

She needed to touch him, feel him with everything she was. Her fingers sliced into his silky hair, flowed along his broad shoulders, and dug into his muscular hips. Piper gasped when Chad drew half her breast into his mouth and clung when he slid a finger inside her to explore her sultry terrain.

"Mmm, nice," he murmured, grazing his lips, his rough chin down her shoulder.

That word, the timbre of his masculine voice, his very touch, was enough to set off seismic rumblings deep inside her. Liberated from her sexual hiatus Piper couldn't stop herself from grinding against his plunging hand, desperate for release.

But he withdrew, though the seismic pressure remained, leaving her teetering precariously on the edge.

With her mind so clouded by sex Piper didn't want to dwell on anything but what they were doing. She was beyond rational thoughts and feelings. Damn the consequences—she needed this man and he needed her. It didn't feel wrong. It might later but at this moment she didn't care.

Piper dropped her head back on the step, it was dead weight anyway. As he raised her hips she shifted willingly, offering herself. He could have her on a platter if that's what he wanted. She just needed him inside her, she needed him now.

Chad smiled down into her glassy eyes, delirious with lust, and entered her.

Piper's orgasm slammed into her so hard she bucked and thrashed violently, inadvertently kicking Chad away. He dropped down to the next tread with a loud thump.

"Holy shit!" He stared at her in surprise as he stood and rubbed his knee.

"Did I hurt you?" she asked, painfully embarrassed.

"I'm fine. You?"

Her blush was so hot it burned. "I'm good."

"I should think so."

"Give me a break, it's been awhile."

"For me, too."

Piper gave him a bashful smile. "Try again?"

Chad chuckled. "Do I dare?"

"If you know what's good for you."

His eyebrows rose along with the corners of his mouth. Without a word he dropped into a pushup position right over her and slowly, teasingly bent his arms to bring his face down to hers. Their kiss deepened and Piper wound her legs around him and pulled him against her.

Yes, oh god yes, she sighed to herself as he slowly entered her a second time. Then she realized to her horror that it was happening again.

"Now!" she screamed and immediately began to quake in his arms.

Astonished, Chad felt her body fighting feverishly to consume and expel him at the same time. Only a committed, determined drive got him completely sheathed and once there all he could do was hold on while Piper's head rocked on the step from side to side as she wailed and laughed like a lunatic. Chad held her close, intimately fused, until her muscles relaxed.

Only when she was still did he lever himself up enough to comb the hair back from her face. "Two," he said shaking his head and grinning. "You're already ahead by two."

"Sorry about that. I guess I'm a little sensitive."

He tried to stop smiling but couldn't. "Think there's any hope for me here?"

She bit her lip and smiled. "I'll be good, I promise. Honestly, this has never happened before."

Chad chuckled, unable to take his eyes off of her. Piper was radiant, a wonder in his arms, soft and wild, absolutely responsive. He moved his hips to withdraw and right before his eyes another heated flush washed over her.

"I'm going," she whimpered, succumbing to another round of spasms.

The speed of Piper's orgasms, not to mention the intense, intimate massage Chad was getting from them was too much for him. Though it would have been nice to draw the act out longer Piper dragged him along fast. He could only manage three solid thrusts before he let out a primal cry of his own.

Chad collapsed onto his left elbow, taking care not to crush her, and tried to regulate his breathing. Piper's arms came up around him and he gazed at her tenderly. She was gloriously naked, still mated to him and his heart took that final defining step and recognized her completely. Before this he only suspected that he loved her—now he knew it for certain.

Then reality elbowed the significant revelation aside and Chad swore. "Fuck fuck fuck!"

Piper, deliriously happy and still drugged with sex, was only mildly interested when she asked, "Anything wrong?"

"Are you on birth control?"

Piper laughed. "Yes. The pill."

He sighed with relief. "Woman, you made me forget myself there."

"Hey, I didn't exactly plan this," she said, pulling his head back by the hair so that he would look at her.

He sighed. "I know. Neither did I, but I'm not sorry."

"Me neither. I guess I wasn't being entirely honest with myself. This was going to happen. Deep down, I knew it and obviously you knew it. So there, it's done. We've gotten that big *when* out of the way and now it's not hanging over us anymore. Curiosity satisfied."

He laughed at her naïveté. "You think it's as simple as that? We have sex once and we're not going to be thinking about it again?"

"I think it might be easier to control ourselves now. We eliminated the tension that was between us."

He kissed her before withdrawing then stretched up. Always the gentleman, he extended a hand and pulled Piper to her feet.

She studied him seriously. "I'm not going to fall in love with you. I think you should know that."

He gave up. "If that's your choice, I don't have a lot to say about it."

She fought a little smile that had a will of its own. "But I want your body again, once more tonight."

Chad considered his next move—briefly. It was something, anyway. "I'd be a fool to pass it up."

"But this will be the last time and the kids will never find out about it. Tomorrow, we go back to being friends, nothing more. Got it?"

"You're the boss." He'd worry about the details later.

Piper reached between his legs and he grew, long and solid in her hand. "You're yummy, Chad. Why don't you show me that nice rug in the living room?"

She led him by the joystick away from the front door and they dropped to the carpet, embarking on a three-hour marathon of lovemaking that neither had ever attempted before.

It was her bladder, or rather a heavy weight pressing on it that woke Piper just before five a.m. Chad's hand was resting on top of her and when she tried to slide it away without waking him it dropped between her legs instead as though it had a mind of its own. She grabbed his wrist and removed it and at the same time felt every sore and abused muscle in her body simultaneously. Chad stirred without opening his eyes and moved his hand back but Piper stopped him.

"Don't. I have to go to the bathroom—now."

His eyes remained closed but he pulled her close and nuzzled her neck.

"I'm serious." She shoved herself away. "I'll be right back."

Chad gradually worked one eye open, followed by the other, and looked around. They'd spent the night on the floor, tumbling across the length of the room and it looked it. Pillows were scattered, magazines were on the floor in tatters after he and Piper rolled into the end table and almost knocked it over. One of the wing chairs was upended and he stared at it for a second until the explanation came back to him. Oh yeah, that one was good. Turning his head to the right he noticed the lamp on the floor. Where the hell was the shade? Shifting he spotted it in the far corner, a good eight feet away. He grinned at how they'd only paused long enough to be sure the bulb wasn't broken before going back on the attack.

The sex last night was manic, furious, and at times they'd slammed together so hard that pain and pleasure mingled. He worried that he would hurt her in a couple of positions but she spurred him on and they collided like asteroids again until finally collapsing, utterly exhausted. Making love to Piper wasn't what he imagined it would be, not even close.

He looked over at the sound of Piper's feet padding over the wood floors. She walked through the archway carrying their clothes.

Chad threw her a lazy contented smile, his heart full of love. "You're beautiful in the morning, all rumpled and sexy."

She smiled and dropped to her knees beside him. Piper leaned down and kissed him. "And you're awfully appealing, too, but I don't have time. I'm already running late."

"How about coming back later?" he asked, rising up on his scuffed elbows with a wince as she pulled her shirt on over her head, ignoring the bra. Chad fished his hand under her shirt and fondled her breast.

Piper wavered, giving his morning hard-on a long conflicted look. "When are the kids coming home?"

"I'm not sure, maybe three?"

She shook her head, her resolve looking shakier by the second. "I don't think I should. We need to take a step back after last night and reestablish our boundaries."

Right, he was going to let her boundaries stand. No way in hell. Chad wrapped his fingers around her ankle and squeezed gently. The suggestive touch made her smile and she looked down at him weakly.

"*This* is the last time," she whispered, her eyes softening. She swung a leg across his hips and lowered herself onto him.

Chad reached up and lifted her shirt, shoving it off over her head so that he could touch her breasts, her neck and face while she rocked in a more gentle rhythm, moving to the peaceful morning sounds of birds and the hum of insects against the screens.

As their tension built, so did their pace. Chad dug his heels into the rug and thrust upwards meeting Piper on her way down. She gasped and shuddered at the deep collision and rode him back to the floor. Gripping his chest hair Piper slid and ground on top of him until finally she sang out like a teakettle.

"Me too," Chad cried, his hands tightening on her breasts as his eyes rolled back.

They climaxed together, connected in every way that two people can be but Chad was the only one who realized how momentous it was. He had no interest in denials as she stretched out on top of him and panted for air. The damp, contrasting curls around their sexes coiled together like vines, a silent testament to the truth she refused to acknowledge.

17

"You're late." Joy called from behind the proofing racks.

Piper rammed her timecard into the machine at a run and almost missed slipping it back in its slot.

"I know." She threw open her locker, hung up her purse, and pulled out her work shoes.

Joy was watching her with a growing sense of wonder.

"You didn't?" she said with disbelief.

Piper stood up, wiggling her feet into her shoes. "Didn't what?"

"Don't play dumb with me. I can see it. You slept with him."

Piper snorted. "I don't know what you're talking about."

Joy laughed, absolutely loving it. "Who's your daddy?"

Piper glared. "Shut up, people can hear you." She saw an older gentleman look up from the French bread display across the counter and she ducked behind the corner.

"Details, girl, I need details."

"What's on the agenda today?"

"Nothing special and you can't put me off that easily."

Piper groaned. "I wouldn't even try but can you wait until our break?"

"I wouldn't count on it."

"Fine," Piper snapped. "Yes, we had sex and it was—there's no other word to describe it—incredible. I'm talking *wow*. I'm still wired. Right now I feel like I could scale Mount Everest or maybe win the Boston Marathon."

"Ooo." Joy quivered like an excited puppy. "He was good, huh?"

Piper looked at her, absolutely serious. "The best I've ever had."

"Oh god."

Piper laughed. "Like I didn't scream *that* over and over last night."

123

"Get out!"

Piper held up a solemn hand. "I swear."

"You're glowing."

"Am I?"

"Like the sun. So, what now?"

Piper went to the sink to wash her hands. "Nothing now."

Joy's mouth fell open and she shook her head. "How can you say that?"

Piper threw her a look at the same time she tossed her paper towel into the garbage. "Because, we're adults, we talked about it and agreed that there would be no repeat performance. We're just friends. Why mess with a good thing?"

Joy rolled her eyes. "I don't get you."

Piper retrieved her mixing bowls and spatulas. "The sex was too hot, too intense." She shook her spatula at Joy. "Some men should come with a warning. You know, like on those fruit pies. Caution: filling is hot. When you eat it you accept the risk. But personally, I'd rather not get burned, thank you very much." Piper turned, unaware she just let her cowardice out of the bag.

It was two in the afternoon when Chad broke down and called her. He'd spent his morning cleaning the house and every minute since she left thinking about her.

Joy answered the phone. She was grinning when she covered the mouthpiece and said, "Piper, it's Big Daddy."

Piper made a face and snatched the phone away from her. "Chad?"

"Yeah, how's it going?"

"Fine. Pretty slow here today."

There was a long pause on the line before he said, "I was hoping you changed your mind. I'll even cook or we can order in. I know the kids wouldn't mind making it a pizza night."

She squeezed her eyes together tight and threw her head back. She didn't appreciate how fast her heart was racing. "I can't and you know it. I think we both need time to cool off, step back. I'll talk to you in a few days, okay?"

After a pause he said, "You know where to find me."

Hearing the disappointment in his voice, Piper cringed.

"Thanks. Bye." She hung up first.

Joy was shocked. "Are you insane?"

"Hey," Piper warned. "I don't need pressure from you, too."

Joy turned away. "Yeah, you are."

It wasn't exactly the dinner Chad planned but it was better than cooking so when his mom brought Missy and Kenny home, Chad took them all out to eat. He wasn't the best company.

Alice, ever perceptive, saw how he struggled to show interest in the kids' chatter. Chad was distant, removed, not himself at all.

Alice grabbed the dessert menu and opened it, sliding it in front of the kids. "How about dessert? What looks good?"

Kenny took the menu and he and his sister put their heads together and started whispering excitedly.

With the kids temporarily distracted, Alice turned to Chad and squeezed his hand.

"You want to talk about it?"

He gave a harsh defeated laugh. "Yes and no. Now's not a good time."

"I'm here."

"I know. Thanks, Mom."

She gave him a quick sympathetic smile and released his hand.

For two days Chad was surly. Normally he didn't have a problem coping with things, even big things, but suddenly even minor issues could set him off. Kenny and Missy did their best to stay out of his way, spending a lot of time playing with their neighborhood friends. Not once did they ask him to make lunch for extra kids. That was a big indicator that they knew he was on the edge. Still, Chad wasn't aware of it until Wednesday morning.

"What's wrong?" he asked the silent kids as they finished their cereal.

"Nothing," they answered in unison.

He didn't buy it. Setting the coffeepot down, he brought the cup to his lips, eyeing them thoughtfully over the rim.

"Are you up to something?" he asked.

"No," they said instantly in two-part harmony, as if they'd rehearsed their lines ahead of time.

Chad excused them with a quick nod and went back to staring out the window and feeling miserable and suspicious. Less than two minutes later he turned at the unexpected sound of little feet coming back and found Missy standing in the doorway looking anxious and unhappy.

"Daddy, are you mad at us?"

The blood drained from his face. "What? Of course not." He held open his arms. "Come here, I'm not mad at you."

Missy ran to him and he picked her up, hugging her close, twisting back and forth and cradling her head against his shoulder.

"Baby, I'm so sorry. I didn't mean to be such a bear. Can you forgive me?"

She nodded, still clinging. Then slowly she leaned back against his arm to study his face. "So what's wrong?"

He smiled sadly. "Someone hurt my feelings."

"Piper?"

His eyebrows went up. "Yeah."

"Doesn't she want to be your friend anymore?"

"I don't think she knows what she wants."

"Do you?"

"Yes."

"Piper?"

"How'd you get to be so smart?"

"*Sex and the City.*"

He laughed. "I forgot."

126

"Can I help?"

"I don't know how. Probably not, but thanks for asking."

She kissed him. "You can put me down now."

"Right." He lowered her to the floor and Missy smiled as she scampered off.

Alice's phone rang.

"Grandma?"

"Missy? What's wrong?"

"You were right. Daddy said he wants Piper."

"He told you that?"

"Uh huh."

"Did he say what happened?"

"No. All he said is that *she* doesn't know what *she* wants—something like that."

Alice's thoughts took her away from the conversation for a moment. Finally Missy broke in with a question.

"Can we help him?"

"I hope so, Missy. I'll have to think about it."

"I will too."

"It can't hurt. Why don't you go play with your friends now okay?"

"Okay."

Piper didn't feel like analyzing precisely why her feet brought her back to the ballpark. Admitting that she wanted to see Chad, as a friend, was all the explanation she wanted. It was as simple as that, really. Not unusual at all to seek out your friends, long for their company, or feel an urge to share their lives.

Nevertheless, when she climbed into the stands with a hot pretzel and a waxed cup of nearly flat Coke she was sneaky about it. She even sat behind a tall man just to use him as an unwitting screen.

When the first team took the field Piper felt a flash of panic. There was nothing familiar about those uniforms. Then her anxiety fled as the first batter walked out of the dugout. Relaxing, she took a bite of her pretzel.

From where she was sitting she couldn't pick Chad out from among his teammates on their bench. The gnawing need to see him again was both painful and unbearable.

The first batter hit a single. The second hitter got him home with a double. The third batter hit right to the shortstop so the runner on second held his base.

When Chad walked out of the dugout and chose a bat along the fence Piper felt an electrical charge shoot through her veins. Looking at him shouldn't feel so good or hurt so bad, should it? The intense brew of emotions in her veins made her want to weep.

Chad faced the plate and dug in with the balls of his feet. He took a couple of powerful practice swings. The force of his swings made Piper breathless. Everything about Chad aroused her, damn it! She shouldn't have come. This was a mistake—a terrible desperate mistake.

She held her breath when he let the first pitch go by. When he fouled the second, she shifted on the bench.

"Come on," she coaxed softly.

The bat connected hard with the third pitch, firing it far into the outfield.

"Yes!" Piper cheered and his bat went flying.

As Chad rounded the bases one after another, pouring on the speed, Piper felt euphoric and exhilarated—her heartbeat an echo of his. Suddenly breathless, she could almost imagine she was right there with him.

Then Chad's foot hit home plate and Piper hunkered down, afraid he'd spot her, but that was a needless fear. He never even looked at the stands because his teammates were waving him over. He slowed to a jog and his hand went up to receive a couple of congratulatory high fives.

Piper leaned forward, searching anxiously for another look at him in that mix of men. Then he reappeared and she breathed easier. Chad pulled off the hard batting helmet and handed it over to another player. He combed his hair back with his fingers and a rush of tenderness swept through Piper like a warm wave.

Shaken and deeply disturbed by her response Piper blanched. *Oh god, what am I doing here?* She couldn't tear her eyes away from Chad as he put his cap back on and sat down on the bench, finally disappearing from her line of sight.

She had to get out of here—now! Seeing him again was beyond torture. Had she completely lost her mind?

Piper set her cup by her feet and turned to look down at the ground. It would be a jump but she was pretty sure she could make it. She spun on the bench and dropped her legs over the back, grabbing hold of the frame. With one big push she sent herself to the grass and fell right on her ass. Brushing herself off as she got to her feet she looked up and realized there was no way she could reach her Coke. She completely misjudged the height. Oh well, c'est la vie.

It was simply chance that Chad happened to look through the fence as he left the dugout. He felt a clutch in his chest when he caught a glimpse of Piper hurrying up the hill away from the field. The urge to run after her was intense, but he couldn't.

He slipped his hand inside his glove and headed to third comforted by the fact that she wanted to see him. It was enough for now that she turned up to watch him play. Even if she wasn't ready to face him yet, at least she came. The laws of attraction were still on his side. He just needed to be patient.

Good luck with that!

18

There was nothing better than giving yourself a minute to bask in your own brilliance and as far as Alice was concerned, her idea was a stroke of genius. It took care of two problems in one bold maneuver.

She held Missy by the hand as they made their way towards the bakery department in Klein's Supermarket.

"If this works out," she whispered to her granddaughter, "I'll buy you a treat. Anything you want."

"It's going to work out, Grandma," Missy said confidently, practically skipping alongside her co-conspirator.

Piper was behind a window at work decorating an enormous graduation cake when she looked up and saw Chad's mother and daughter watching her through the glass.

Oh great.

Piper flashed a quick insincere smile at them then continued with the border. When that was finished she started placing the roses she made earlier into the corners. Missy watched with rapt fascination. Responding to it, Piper gave her a more genuine smile this time then picked up the bag of green frosting and added more curling leaves. She could hear Missy's "oh" of wonder through the glass.

The last thing Piper did was put the congratulations message across the top in elegant script.

Missy rose up on her tiptoes to watch and when Piper was finished she turned the cake around and lifted the back edge so the little girl could see the finished product.

"That's really pretty Piper," Missy exclaimed. "Can you make me a cake, too?"

Piper smiled and stepped out from behind the glass so she could talk with them. "Maybe," she said, grinding her fist into the knot in her lower back. "You should look at our book over there."

"You're an artist."

Piper laughed. "Hardly."

Alice spoke up. "Don't you teach classes anymore?"

"I will when summer is over. Right now lots of people want cakes for parties and weddings. I'm needed here."

"You make wedding cakes, too?" Missy asked, obviously impressed.

"All the time."

"I have a loose tooth," Missy announced out of the blue.

Piper laughed at the unexpected change in topic. "Is that right? Which one?"

Missy wiggled an upper front tooth. "Daddy says I'll be able to whistle when it falls out."

"Can't you whistle now?"

"No," she admitted sadly.

"Well I wouldn't worry too much about that. I can't whistle either."

"Really?"

Piper held up her hand. "I swear."

Hearing that she wasn't the only one seemed to please the girl.

Alice broke in. "Piper, I was hoping I could ask a favor."

Piper felt her stiff spine clench even tighter. Fantastic. She was going to need a long hot soak tonight. "Oh yeah?" she asked warily.

"The thing is, Chad's got tickets to a concert on Friday and I was hoping you could go in my place. I actually made other plans that frankly I'd much rather keep. I'm the wrong generation for that sort of music anyway and the tickets are already paid for. I have a feeling you'll enjoy it far more than I would."

"I don't know," she hedged. "Doesn't he have other friends he can ask?"

Alice frowned. "Couples. Who do you think he should leave out? It's *one* ticket. If you don't go he's going to have to eat the cost of it."

Piper looked around helplessly. She hated being railroaded into things. To her growing annoyance, Joy was working against her, too, nodding emphatically and giving her meaningful, expressive looks with her eyes.

Piper sighed and turned back to Alice. "Does Chad even know you're asking me to go instead?"

"Not yet, but he will. Don't you worry, I'll take care of everything."

Piper's inner demon went to work, wearing her down even more. What could happen at a concert? They'd hardly get a chance to talk over the music anyway and the crowd would keep things from getting out of hand, right?

Could she trust herself with Chad again? Alone, she had her doubts, but in this situation—probably.

"Fine, I guess I can."

Alice beamed at her. "Wonderful. I'll tell him to call you and work out the details." She looked over at her granddaughter who was paging through the binder of pictures. "Missy, come over here. It's time to tell us what you want."

Missy skipped over and grinned up at Piper like a girl with a happy secret.

When the two Thomas's left with a bag full of goodies, Joy sidled over and slapped Piper across the arm. "Do you even know who's in town on Friday?"

"Oww," Piper said, rubbing her bicep. "No, but I'm sure you'll tell me."

"I can't believe he was able to get tickets! That concert was sold out as soon as it was announced. I would kill to trade places with you."

"I give, who is it?"

"Green Swizzle Wooster!"

Piper gasped. "Shut up!"

"I kid you not!"

"I totally love them."

"Duh!"

When Chad called later that night they both played it casual. Neither mentioned his ball game, which helped. They kept the conversation brief, sticking to relevant details for Friday. Since Chad still hadn't been to Piper's apartment she thought it would be best if she met him at his house again. This time she planned to cut it close so he wouldn't have time to invite her in then afterwards she'd be gone like the wind.

Piper found Joy's enthusiasm for a concert she wasn't even going to see beyond comprehension.

Friday afternoon was especially bizarre.

"Do you know what would look great on you tonight?" Joy asked.

"I give," Piper said wearily.

"I have this little black lacy shell of a top from Victoria's."

"I've seen it."

"You could wear it with those black leather jeans you have. Oh, and your boots. I'll let you borrow it."

"Joy, I don't think that's the right tone for tonight."

"Of course it is."

"Would you stop? I mean it, just stop. Please. I don't want to confuse Chad with mixed signals. You know how hard I've been working to back up the train so it doesn't help that you want me to suddenly start waving him through the tunnel."

"Nice metaphor."

"I'm serious. The last thing I want to do is torture the poor guy. I like him too much. It would be unbelievably cruel."

"What if he'd like to see you dressed that way?"

"That's beside the point."

"I really think you're insane."

"Said the pot to the kettle."

"And you're childish."

"I told you I was reverting."

Piper showed up at the Thomas house wearing a conservative skirt and sweater set finished off with a pair of low sensible heels. Joy would be seriously disappointed in her but not very surprised.

Missy answered the doorbell wearing a sweet little sundress. Her hair was pulled back by matching butterfly combs. She gasped when she saw Piper. "Wow, you look so pretty."

"So do you. I love your barrettes. Did you do your own hair?"

"Daddy did it but I helped."

Piper could just picture Chad sitting behind his daughter with a brush in his hand and barrettes in his mouth while he fiddled with all that hair. Don't go there, she warned herself. Too many emotional land mines—steer clear of the sweet scenes.

Piper stepped onto the tiles and shut the door.

"Looks like you have a big night, too, huh?"

"We do." Missy grinned.

"And you still have your tooth I see."

Missy wiggled it for her. They both turned as Kenny came clumping down the staircase dressed in a polo shirt and chinos. He looked ridiculously handsome even with the sour scowl.

"Oh, look at you," Piper said, melting at Chad's little copy.

Kenny didn't have a chance to complain about dressing up because Chad walked out of his bedroom and Piper was lost, and with every step Chad took on the way down to her she lost a little more to him. Then Chad smiled and Piper felt it in her belly, in her chest and it wrenched.

"Good, you're right on time," he said.

Piper couldn't tear her eyes away from his chin, his jaw when he spoke. She remembered, vividly, how he skimmed his face over her tender bare skin, roughing it, teasing it. She knew now how his stubble felt under her tongue, between her thighs, behind her knees, brushing over her neck and shoulders. Then Chad smiled and she remembered his front teeth drawing slowly across her hard nipples. Oh shit, she was a goner. Damn it, she was totally screwed.

"I think we should get going," Chad announced, unaware of the thoughts swirling in Piper's head.

Everyone climbed into his car. Piper assumed that they would drop the kids off somewhere en route but Missy and Kenny rode all the way into Lewiston with them. When they drove past the civic center without slowing Piper looked back, watching the crowds funnel inside. She turned to Chad with a look of confusion and he smiled without offering an explanation.

Eventually they joined a line of cars blocks away from the civic center and were eventually waved into a parking ramp by attendants with lighted batons.

"We're here," Chad announced. The kids went wild.

"Dare I ask?" Piper said.

"Just wait and see."

Missy climbed out of the car. "Yeah, it's a big surprise."

"Your dad is big on surprises," said Piper, the sarcasm leaking out unbidden.

Chad grinned, clearly amused, and they set off for the theater.

Walking down the ramp Missy moved to Piper's side and took her hand. Ever so subtly she began to maneuver Piper closer to her dad. Chad looked over with raised eyebrows and Piper shrugged, nodding at Missy.

He chuckled. "Ah." His sweet little fixer was at work.

Just inside the theater Piper finally saw the posters.

"The Fruit Bowl followed by the Dancing Bear Band?" she asked, looking at Chad in shock.

He gave her a huge grin, his eyes absolutely sparkling. "Think of the Fruit Bowl as those Fruit of the Loom guys set to music."

"They dance, too," said Kenny.

Missy pointed to the poster. "I like the grapes."

"No way, the banana is best," said Kenny.

This was the most bizarre conversation Piper had ever tried to follow. Her obvious confusion made Chad laugh. "The banana sings bass."

"Oh," she said vaguely. "Now it makes sense." She rolled her eyes. Oh well, now that she was here might as well get into the spirit of the thing.

An usher led them to their aisle and Kenny took off down the row, dropping into the first of their seats.

"Ken, we're not going to climb over you so get up and move all the way down to number twenty-four," said Chad.

Kenny hauled himself up and moved down three more seats.

Missy drew back, pushing Piper in behind her dad so they'd have to sit together. She followed last, claiming the outside seat and kicking her feet merrily as she watched the theater fill.

Admittedly, the concert wasn't exactly what Piper was expecting but she was astonished at how enjoyable the show actually was. Aside from the silly costumes and creative lyrics, the groups were obvious professionals. Some of the music was particularly beautiful and the harmonies of the Fruit Bowls could rival any Motown group she ever heard.

During the intermission they hit the restrooms by twos, the girls and boys separating to go to the appropriate door. Piper was washing her hands and checking her make-up in the mirror when Missy walked up behind her, shaken and pale.

Piper spun around in alarm. "Sweetie, what's wrong?"

Missy gave Piper a damaged smile, showing the gap in her pink gums.

Piper sagged with relief. "Do you have it?"

The little girl opened her hand and held out her tiny perfect tooth. Piper pulled a Kleenex out of her purse and folded it carefully inside.

Giving Missy an encouraging smile, Piper said, "My dad's a dentist, you know. So I know all about these things. Everything is perfectly fine."

The guys were already in their seats when the girls got back just before the lights dimmed for the second half of the show.

Piper leaned close to Chad and whispered, "Missy has something to show you."

His eyebrows went up and he leaned forward to look at his daughter. "Missy, what is it, honey?"

Missy smiled at him.

"Hey!" Chad said with a smile of his own. "You look like a jack o'lantern. You didn't swallow it, did you?"

"No." Missy held out the Kleenex. Chad carefully felt for the tooth inside.

"Why don't I hold onto this? Then, when we get home, we'll put it under your pillow, okay?"

"Okay."

Chad slipped the precious tissue into his breast pocket and patted it protectively. Piper melted.

19

The Dancing Bear Band didn't just take the stage, they *seized* it and got the kids worked up by their antics before they even played a single note.

As they broke into their first number Piper and Chad both moved to claim the armrest between them at exactly the same time. He beat her to it but it was a shallow victory. With an apologetic look he turned his palm up and held his hand open. Piper took a deep breath and laid her arm on top of his and when their fingers meshed he curled their hands into one.

Missy laid her head against Piper's arm and smiled up at her devotedly. Piper's heart softened even more and the girls ended up holding hands too. All three made a chain and remained connected for the rest of the performance. Overcome by the intimacy and affection surrounding her, Piper was in no position to judge the quality of The Dancing Bear Band. She hardly heard them.

When they pulled into the garage just over an hour later Kenny and Missy were fast asleep, slumped against their car doors. Chad and Piper opened the back doors carefully, reaching in to catch the limp children before they dropped out. Chad looked across the seat and found Piper. Their eyes met and held for a moment as they shared a warm smile then they reached over the sleeping kids and released their seatbelts.

Chad carried his son and Piper carried his daughter into the house, up the stairs, and into their bedrooms.

Missy's nightlight helped Piper avoid tripping over the array of toys as she carried her to the bed. The girl's nightgown was draped across the foot of the bed. Piper set her down and gently peeled

Missy out of her pretty outfit; her shoes, tights, and dress. The combs fell out on their own and Piper moved them to the little table out of the way before laying Missy on her back and working her arms, one at a time, into her pajama sleeves.

Piper was just trying to figure out how to get the nightgown over Missy's lolling head when Chad came in. He hurried over and lifted Missy enough so that Piper could slip her head through the neck hole and together they worked it down without waking her. Then Chad stepped back and let Piper pull the covers over his daughter.

"I almost forgot," Chad whispered suddenly and pulled his wallet out of his back pocket. He sorted through the bills and extracted a dollar, slipping it under the pillow.

"A buck? Seriously?" Piper whispered.

"Cost of living increase."

Piper smiled, took one last parting look at the sleeping girl, then turned and stumbled right over a stuffed hippo. Chad's hand shot out and he caught her by the arm before she could fall over anything else. She gave him a silent nod of thanks and walked out. He followed, closing the door quietly behind him.

They stopped in the hall.

Chad looked tired but content. "Thanks for helping tonight."

Piper gave a muted laugh. "Thanks for the concert."

"Was it what you expected?" His eyes were dancing now.

"Oh yeah. I owe your mother."

He chuckled softly. "Come on. Let's get out of here before we wake them."

Piper followed him downstairs and around to the kitchen. Chad bent smoothly and picked up Piper's purse from the floor where she dropped it when she carried Missy inside.

"I've never undressed, or dressed for that matter, a child before," she said taking a stool at the counter.

"It didn't show."

She shook her head. "You came in just in time."

He poured them each a glass of juice and slid one across to her.

Piper took hers gratefully. The dry air in the theater had left her incredibly thirsty.

"Is my time in the doghouse over?" Chad asked.

She looked up. "You were never in the doghouse."

"Felt like it."

"I'm sorry. That's what I wanted to avoid." Then she smiled. "Your family is conspiring against us."

"You maybe."

"Don't."

"I'm sorry." The last fragments of the charming magical night faded, leaving awkwardness in its place.

"I should probably get going."

"I'll walk you out."

"I wish you wouldn't."

He looked at her for a full minute before nodding. "Okay."

"Will you kiss the kids for me?" she asked, picking up her purse.

"Glad to."

She smiled, sincerely. "They're really great."

With that, she turned and left. Chad remained, leaning back against the counter he finished his juice. He didn't shut off the lights and head up to bed until Piper was long gone.

20

Piper could hardly wake up for her shift on Saturday morning. She swayed bleary eyed as she clocked in and couldn't get to the coffee pot fast enough.

Joy waited impatiently with her own cup in her hand. "So, how was the concert? I need details."

Piper gave an enormous yawn, blinking her tired tears away. "I think I agree with Kenny. The banana is the best, though the grapes are pretty awesome."

"Huh?"

Piper smirked. "I was shanghaied."

"But what's with the fruit?"

"Chad's a heterosexual."

"Quit fucking with me. Need I remind you it's five in the effing morning?"

"We did not go to see Green Swizzle Wooster."

"You're kidding."

"Do I look like I'm kidding?"

"And the banana?"

"He sings bass."

Joy started to giggle, then broke into a hearty laugh. "I don't even *want* to know about the grapes."

"Good."

"So ..."

"Yeah. It was a kiddie concert with Kenny and Missy. We had a hell of a time."

"Anything else I should know about?"

"Zip, unless you're asking if I'm going to get even with you for pushing me into this."

"Nope, I'm good. How are you?"

"Talk to me at ten and I'll know by then—hopefully."

Some days it just doesn't pay to get out of bed. Thinking back, Piper couldn't recall a more hellish shift. It was going to take a good night's sleep just to recover from this one. The snafu that really made it memorable was the horrifying stop motion instant when the special order birthday cake she just finished took a heart-stopping header right off the edge of the counter and flipped face down onto the floor.

Poor Joy was so distraught when she pulled the sheet trays back a second too late that Piper could barely console her.

The good news was that they always baked extra cakes for the self-serve case. Piper ran and grabbed one of those then carefully scraped it clean, sliding the roses and piped edges off of it before transforming the replacement into one with a rock star theme at record speed. She was just closing up the box when the customer stopped back.

The woman asked to see it first and Piper held her breath as she presented the box. To her relief the customer fawned over the rushed copy never suspecting that the original was now an unidentifiable mass in the garbage can.

Four o'clock and free at last. Piper stopped at the deli for a roast beef and provolone sandwich before heading home.

Shaken when she dozed off in the shower, Piper went right to bed and fell into an exhausted sleep.

At four a.m. Piper's alarm clock went off, startling her so badly she almost fell out of bed when she took a swing at the button on top. Then, rolling over with a moan, Piper weighed her need for more sleep against the advisability of getting her ass out of bed. Her responsibilities won out. They always did.

Joy yawned. "I'll bet sometimes you almost miss working nights."

"Almost." Piper looked at the clock and nodded lethargically. It was only five-thirty and already they were three coffees in and if they didn't snap out of it, they'd never get anything done. "But I think I slept too much."

Joy gave her a queer look. "Too much? How can you sleep too much?"

"You've never done that? You know, when you go to bed too early and sleep right through and the next day, you feel even more tired?"

"Girl, you're nuts. I've never heard of anything so crazy."

Piper rolled her burning eyes. "Just get First Methodist's order done."

Joy shifted the tray of rising rolls in the warmer. "Do you ever wonder why there's not a second or a twentieth or even a fifty-first Methodist or Congregationalist? I think nobody wants to admit they're not first. It's all about inferiority."

"Philosophy before six in the morning? I'm blessed."

"You've got that right. I have to apply my minor somewhere and I don't share these observations with just anyone, you know." Joy started whipping up chocolate frosting. "By the way, I wanted to tell you that Dom and I are having a party on Saturday. We want you to come."

"You know I don't do parties."

"Just this once. You can bring Chad. I've been dying to meet him."

"I'll have to get back to you on that."

"You better."

Chad called Piper that afternoon and invited her over. When she hesitated he asked, "Are you already busy?"

"Yes and no. I was going to go home and take a nap."

"Tough day?"

"Not as bad as yesterday but we were busy and my internal

clock still hasn't adjusted to my insane hours." She tried and failed to stifle a yawn.

Chad chuckled. "Go home and get some sleep and maybe when you wake up you'll feel like stopping over."

"I'm not making any promises."

"Understood. Now get some rest."

It was after six in the evening when Piper peeled her eyes open and panicked. She meant to call Chad and beg off sooner. She didn't want him holding dinner for a no-show.

He picked up after the second ring.

"Hey, I'm sorry it took me so long to call you back," she said.

"No problem. I knew what was going on. Are you feeling better?"

"Still a little groggy but yes, I'm better."

"Good. Hamburgers are just about to go on the grill, do you like onions?"

"What?" Her pass on the dinner invite was getting away from her.

"Onions—yea or nay?"

"Nay." She had no resolve. How infuriating.

"Throw something on and hurry over."

She looked down at her naked body and wondered if the man had psychic abilities.

"Do I need to bring anything?"

"Just a sunny disposition."

"I think it's still boxed up in the closet."

"Chipper works too if you can't find sunny."

"Damn, chipper's in the strainer by the sink. I needed to rinse it out."

"Just give it a good shake. Problem solved."

Piper laughed. "Fine, you've got me. I'll be there shortly."

"Drive safely."

The second Piper hung up she realized Chad's warning wasn't an idle one. He'd learned the hard way not to take traffic hazards lightly.

Naturally he'd worry about her until she got there in one piece.

They played whiffle ball in the backyard then everyone went inside and settled in front of the television. The kids put on an animated movie while Piper and Chad made themselves comfortable on the sofa.

"So what does your mom do, Chad?"

"Nothing," he said with an idle shrug.

She laughed. "Nice work if you can get it."

"What I meant is Mom doesn't have to work. My parents owned a couple of small banks. Mom was the not-so-silent partner but it was my dad who ran them. He was good at it."

"And you didn't want to go into the family business?"

He chuckled and the kids shushed him from the floor. "No. My dad was an accountant slash businessman and I thought it was too tame for me. I wanted to get into something more manly."

"And you did."

He shook his head, grinning. "It started out that way. I got down and dirty with the best of them but I found out that I have my dad's knack after all and my talents were better served by organizing. Now I'm an accountant slash businessman even if I occasionally wear a hard hat and dump dirt out of my shoes."

"But are you happy?"

"Very."

"The test of a vocation is the love of the drudgery it involves." Piper smiled. "Logan Pearsall Smith. It's one of my favorite quotes."

"I like it."

"So where's your dad? I haven't met him yet."

"You won't. He had a heart attack eight months before Chelsea died. It was an undiagnosed condition—a birth defect. If Dad was a more active person it would have shown up a lot sooner."

"I'm so sorry."

"Thanks. Anyway, after he died, Mom reconsidered a couple

of offers on the banks and eventually sold them. Now they're branches of Republic. Part of the sale included stocks in the parent company so she gets by just fine." Chad stood up and looked at her. "I'm going to get something to drink—you want anything?"

"Make me an offer."

"I made a pitcher of cran-something or other before you got here."

"Can I have some?" Kenny asked from the floor.

"Not in here," Chad said. "If you two want juice you have to drink it in the kitchen."

Missy paused the movie and everyone went for juice. The kids were the only ones to go back into the living room. Chad and Piper sat at the kitchen table and continued their talk.

"Tell me a little about your family," Chad said. "Any siblings?"

"My older brother Bill lives in Portland with his wife Julia. They have two kids in college but then he was a teen when I was born so we never really had a chance to get close before he flew the nest."

"What about your parents?"

"My dad is a dentist, Dr. Frost." She smiled. "He has a small office in Martin Heights and my mom used to help out with scheduling until my grandma moved in with them. She needed a lot of care so they set up a little apartment on the first floor and Mom went into nursing fulltime. When Grandma died Mom didn't go back to work. Dad didn't really need her at the office by then. Sometimes I worry about my mom. She seems a little lost without something to occupy her."

Loud music announced the end of the movie and Chad excused himself to look in on kids.

"Time for bed," he said. "Upstairs and brush your teeth."

They both whined and complained but Chad stood firm. "I don't want to argue. It's bed time."

"But its summer vacation and we want to watch TV with you. Besides, Piper's still here." Kenny gave his dad the full treatment, pleading eyes and all. "Please Dad, please? We're not even tired yet."

Missy nodded, agreeing wholeheartedly with her brother.

After a thoughtful pause Chad relented. "Fine, go upstairs and put on your pajamas and brush your teeth first."

The excited kids hit the stairs running.

"You're giving in to them?" Piper asked, coming up behind him.

Chad turned. "I'm going to make a point."

Intrigued, she eyed him expectantly.

He smiled. "What's worse than not getting what you want?"

"Getting it."

"Precisely."

When the kids came back they were beaming and even when Chad explained the conditions their happiness over their modest victory never wavered.

"Okay, here's the deal, you can watch television with us but you can't complain about what's on and you don't get to go to bed until I say so, understood?"

The kids thought that sounded fair and Kenny actually scoffed at the suggestion that he'd even ask. Chad turned on a late baseball game and the kids sat on the floor sharing smiles back and forth, assuming they won.

"Maybe I should leave," Piper whispered discretely to Chad.

"No, you're going to want to watch this," he said with a conspiratorial grin.

For the next twenty minutes the kids hung in there but after that they were both fighting hard to keep their eyes open. Only during the blaring commercials did they seem to revive but it was short lived. For the adults sitting behind them, watching the kids was far more entertaining than the game.

It was easy to tell when one of them started nodding off because their heads would bob a few times first before finally slumping heavily. That's when Chad would switch the station and startle the kids awake with loud commercials.

They didn't make it an hour before they were pleading to go to bed.

"You don't want to go up now," Chad said in disbelief. "There's another inning to go."

Yes they did, but they shut up about it for another ten minutes. That was as long as they could last before the sniffling started.

Piper turned on Chad with a tortured look but he shook his head and whispered, "Not yet."

Only when their crying had turned into actual blubbering did Chad mute the television and pretend to be confused. "What's wrong?"

"We want to go to bed," they whimpered brokenly.

"I don't understand. You begged me to let you stay up late. We argued about it."

"We don't want to anymore," Kenny sobbed. His face was red and wet.

Piper's heart was breaking. She looked at Chad helplessly, biting her tongue. It was difficult not to interfere.

"Missy, you don't want to go to bed already do you?" Chad asked her gently.

She nodded. "I'm sooo tired. Please, Daddy, can we go to bed?"

Chad's voice was grave but his eyes were compassionate. "Are we going to fight about bedtimes anymore?"

The kids sniffled and shook their heads.

"Okay. Off to bed."

Missy rushed her dad for a hug, leaving an undecided Kenny to figure out what he wanted to do. Then he rushed forward, too, gratitude overwhelming his reticence. Piper watched, her emotions shifting between relief and tenderness.

Then Missy released her dad and gave Piper a big hug. Surprised and deeply moved, Piper kissed the girl's cheek and wished her sweet dreams.

Kenny fidgeted for a minute before throwing himself at her next but he bolted after his sister before Piper could give him a kiss, too.

Chad and Piper stared at each other, so stunned they both

needed a moment to collect themselves.

When he finally trusted himself to speak Chad asked, "Well? How'd I do?"

Her eyes were sparkling when she smiled. "That was brilliant. How did you know that would work?"

"My dad did the same thing to me when I was a kid. It made an impression."

"This was a learning experience for me. I like your style, Chad. I'm sure it would be easier to yell at them but by doing what you did I doubt you'll have to fight over this again."

"No, they'll just find something else to throw at me."

"I suppose that's parenting, but I have to say, you're doing a really good job at it."

"Thanks."

"That said, I need to get going."

"Yeah, I've got to work tomorrow."

"I don't," she said, gloating.

"Hey, you wouldn't want to hang out with Missy and Kenny tomorrow night, would you?"

"What's going on?"

"I have a game and my mom has a date so she cancelled on me."

"Do you want us there with you?"

"That's up to you three."

"I suppose I can ask them what they want to do."

"So you'll do it?"

"Sure, why not? I don't have anything better planned."

"Great. Dinner has to be at five if I'm going to get to the field on time."

"I'm bringing dinner so have the kids watching for me around four."

"You don't have to feed us."

"I want to."

21

Piper stopped at the store and picked up a bag of groceries. She was going to hold a little class in the Thomas kitchen.

Missy insisted on cooking so Piper had her watching the chicken breasts over a low flame while she set up Kenny at the table with a big bowl. He thoroughly enjoyed shredding lettuce into it, a natural at destruction. When it was time to flip the breasts Piper stood behind Missy and helped.

"Very good, see that color, that's what you want."

Kenny was finished and Piper picked up a few stray pieces of green and tossed them into the bowl then put it aside.

"Now I have something even better for you," she said, trying to create a little excitement in him.

"What?"

"You're going to take this grapefruit spoon and pull all the stems off the strawberries. Watch how this works." She inserted the point under the stem and twisted it free.

"Hey, I can do that," he reached for the spoon.

"Be careful not to squeeze the strawberries, they squish really easily."

The chicken was done so she shut off the flame and put the breasts onto a shallow tray. "Get two forks, okay?" She sent Missy to a drawer. When Kenny saw his sister shredding the chicken he wanted to trade jobs. They compromised. Missy would do two breasts, Kenny would do two. The kids were impressed when they saw how fast and perfectly Piper sliced the tomatoes and onions.

"Smells good," Chad said, walking out of his office.

"Dinner's about ready, why don't you go wash your hands," said Piper.

He smiled at all of them, stopping by Kenny to watch him

industriously pulling the last of the chicken apart with forks. Next he wandered over to Missy and watched her put the final strawberry on top of her yogurt parfaits.

"That's beautiful, honey," he told her and kissed the top of her head.

"Thanks. It's a parfait, like in the movie *Shrek*."

"Cool. Is there anything I can do to help?" he asked Piper.

"No, we're all set."

He went to the sink and washed while the others set the table. When they sat down, Piper demonstrated for the kids how to make a wrap. Chad was amazed at how willing they were to eat what they prepared, especially finicky Missy.

When Piper went on and on about how pretty the tomatoes looked on top of the lettuce Missy took a few and placed them carefully into her wrap. She admired it for a moment herself then surprised her dad by actually eating it. Apparently kids would try anything if you knew how to sell it. He could learn from this.

Over dinner the kids decided they'd rather stay home and play than go to the field. Chad went upstairs to change, calling a quick good-bye on his way out.

Back in the kitchen Piper organized a cleaning party and together they tidied up in no time. She felt like Mary Poppins but they didn't know the movie when she mentioned it.

"What do you mean you've never seen it? It's a classic," said Piper in surprise.

Kenny and Missy looked at each other and shrugged.

"I'll have to rent it and we'll watch it together. How does that sound?"

Both kids were on board with that plan.

Once the work was done Kenny went to play with his friend next door.

Missy looked to Piper. "What do you want to do?"

Piper grinned. "I want to play with your castle."

Missy's jaw dropped and she asked excitedly, "Really?"

"Really."

Piper noticed the huge castle sitting on the floor in Missy's room when she put her to bed after the concert and ever since she'd been dying to take a closer look at it. She would have loved something like that when she was a girl.

They dragged it out into the middle of the floor, tossing toys onto the bed to make room, and opened it up. Piper percolated with excitement when the dolls and animals toppled out.

"Can I play with her?" she asked, picking up a princess.

Missy nodded. "Sure. This one's my favorite." She held up her own princess doll and they cleared out the mess and set up the scene.

Piper laughed. "Oh cool, a wizard!"

"He's Kenny's. Here, you need Reginald," Missy handed Piper a caped prince. "He's Belinda's boyfriend."

"I have Belinda?"

"Uh huh."

"Where did you get these?" Piper asked, loving everything more and more.

"Daddy bought me the castle and Grandma found me all the people. I have some of Kenny's action figures in here too but they're too small and they don't bend like these."

Missy shifted through the toys for a second. "Look, this is Prince Steven. He's going to marry Princess Marigold." She showed off her prince, dressed in gorgeous deep blue with silver embellishments.

Piper carefully inspected Reginald's elaborate burgundy costume with its gold detailing and puffed sleeves. She pulled the matching velvet cape up to admire the satin lining. His tights absolutely delighted her. She giggled. "I love these."

"Grandma had the outfits made special for me. The clothes that the dolls came with were all wrong."

It didn't take the girls long before they decided to put on a royal ball but then Kenny came back and picked up the dragon puppet, unleashing terror, upturning tables, chairs, even the thrones before flying off with the damsels clamped in his mouth. He was threatening to drop them from his perch, a dangerous height, which was actually Missy's dresser, but Prince Steven and his best friend Reginald were able to rescue both princesses from the evil beast and return them to the safety of the castle. They closed the toys inside after that and Piper helped Missy push the castle against the wall.

"Can I come back and play castle again sometime?" Piper asked, walking downstairs with the kids.

"I'd love that." Missy smiled up at her. "When I get married I'm going to be a princess just like Marigold."

Kenny snorted. "Big surprise."

Piper winked at the girl. "Well I think that's a great idea."

"And you can come too and wear a cone hat like Belinda's."

"I might have to do that." Piper grinned.

"But I get the crown," Missy said quite seriously.

"Of course."

The kids were already in bed when Chad got home. He walked into the living room and found Piper sleeping on the couch. The peaceful look on her face drew him over. All he wanted to do right then was sit quietly and simply watch over her while she slept, like he did sometimes with his kids. Like he used to do with Chelsea. But Piper woke up before he even reached her.

"You're back," she said groggily, dragging herself up.

"I am."

"Did you win?"

He sat on the arm of the couch by her feet. "Just barely. How did it go here?"

She smiled. "I want to come back and play again."

He laughed. "Anytime."

Piper swung her legs around and stood up with a stretch. "I had fun."

"I'm glad. Thanks for coming over."

"You're welcome."

He walked her to the door and saw her out, aching with the need to touch her again.

Piper climbed into her car feeling conflicted because he didn't try to kiss her. She couldn't tell if she was more relieved or disappointed. Her money was on disappointed.

22

Joy and Piper both turned when one of Klein's stockers came running behind their glass cases, breathless and excited.

"What's up, Rhonda?" Joy asked.

"You've got to check out the guy at the self-serve donuts. I'm running a temperature here."

Piper and Joy hurried to the display case and peeked over the top.

"Oh baby, you were right," Joy agreed, appreciating the view.

Piper knew that ass. When he bent a little for a third bakery box the other two nearly swooned in ecstasy.

"If the front matches the back I'm gonna faint," said Rhonda.

Piper grinned. "It does."

They both turned to stare at her.

"You know him?" Joy asked.

"That's Chad."

"Oh my god, *that's* your Big Daddy?"

Piper let the possessive Big Daddy remark slide. She didn't want to deny it and then be forced to watch assertive Rhonda hit on him. She liked the woman. She'd hate to have to kill her.

"Now my imagination is fried—did you just call him *Big Daddy?*" Rhonda asked with a moan.

Joy chuckled. "So the legend goes."

"Knock it off," Piper hissed. "He's going to hear you two."

Just then he turned and walked right towards them with his stack of boxes.

"Honest to god, my knees are knocking together. I've got to go." Rhonda scurried off, giving Chad a long appraising look before she disappeared down the cereal aisle.

"Hi Piper, how's it going?" he asked with a devastating smile, setting his boxes on top of the case.

Joy cleared her throat and gave Piper a nudge, then a sharp prod with her elbow.

Piper hip checked her right back. "Good. Chad, this is my friend Joy."

He turned his stunning wattage on Joy and she lit up like Broadway. "Hey there, Chad, it's nice to finally meet you. Did Piper tell you about my party yet? This Saturday?"

"No," he said carefully, looking at Piper.

Piper kicked the side of Joy's foot. "I was going to last night but I forgot," she fudged and turned to Joy hoping she'd take a hint. "Shouldn't you check on that thing in the oven?"

Joy smiled sweetly, knowing it would annoy Piper. "Nuh uh. It's fine."

Piper sighed and looked at Chad. "So do you want to go with me?"

"Love to."

"Anytime after seven," Joy added with a big smile. "Piper knows the way."

"Great."

Piper looked over Chad's shoulder. "Did you leave us any donuts?"

He laughed. "A few. I'm just on my way over to the work site and I thought I'd bring the crew a treat."

"Aw, that's so sweet," Joy gushed, half in love with him already.

"Don't work too hard, ladies." He picked up his boxes. "I'll see you Saturday, Joy."

"Looking forward to it Chad."

"I'm going to get you for this," Piper hissed.

"Yeah yeah, and my little dog too," said Joy, waving the threat off before finally turning and laughing at Piper.

"What?"

"You know when I said you were crazy? I was *so* wrong. Honey, I'm serious—seek help."

Piper called Chad that night to make the arrangements.

"So I'll pick you up at seven then," she said.

"I'll be ready."

When Piper pulled into Chad's driveway on Saturday night, he was out his front door before she even put the car into park. He locked up behind him then walked around to the passenger side to get in beside her. His smile, his greeting, and the smell of his aftershave were as effective as a head injury at scrambling her brains. It was a challenge just trying to behave normally when every cell in her body was suddenly on high alert.

Piper forced herself calm. "Were you watching for me?"

"No, I just know how you time things so I was ready."

"Great." She was already predictable? Not so great.

It was an awkward ride but at least it wasn't a long trip. Piper wasn't exactly immune to the man and his damned aftershave was seriously beginning to piss her off. She tried to ignore it. Fat chance. Piper glanced at her window, desperate to breathe outside air even if it meant choking on exhaust fumes and dealing with the smell of hot baking asphalt. At least she'd be safe from that seductive masculine scent of his but unfortunately if she opened the windows she'd completely screw up her hair. Life was so unfair.

Piper parked along the curb in front of Joy and Dom's house.

"It looks like we're the first ones here," Chad said, none too happily.

Piper pulled the keys out of the ignition. "Does that pose a problem for you?"

He looked at her. "No, just making an observation."

"Come on then."

Joy threw open the front door and let out a squeal. "Fantastic!" She hooked her arm through Chad's and dragged him through the house and into the kitchen, leaving Piper to follow after them like a stray puppy.

The table and counter were so loaded with snacks you couldn't see the surfaces. A large punch bowl dominated one corner of the table.

Joy pointed to it. "Spiked, of course. Should have a nice kick."

Piper grinned. "Naturally."

"Might as well help yourselves. There's something for every taste here; sweet, salty, sour, and hot." Joy waved towards the various plates and bowls as she went. "Oh, and there's a keg in the garage and a stack of glasses—already tapped," she added looking at Chad specifically.

"Thanks, but punch will be fine for me," he said. "Piper?"

"Sure, I'll have some punch."

They all turned at the sound of the doorbell.

"And we're off," Joy said excitedly. "You two got this?"

"No problem," said Piper.

"Cool. I've got to answer that because Dom's getting dressed."

Joy took off and Chad picked up the ladle and a plastic cup. He gave Piper the first glass then filled a second.

"Let's get this party started," he said with a grin and tapped his cup against hers.

"Cheers." Piper raised her glass and held it, waiting for Chad to take the first swallow. Knowing her friends, there was no reason they both had to play guinea pig.

Chad's eyes were tearing when he came up choking and sputtering. Now she felt guilty. She probably should have given him a little warning.

"Whoa," he gasped. "She wasn't kidding about the kick." He fought to breathe through the burn, his hand on his chest.

"Damn, now I *have* to taste it." Piper's face fell. "This is the true measure of friendship right here. I want you to witness this."

Chad blotted his eyes and watched with a comical face as Piper slowly brought her cup to her lips. One whiff of the vapors was enough to make her eyes water but still she took a dainty sip.

"Oh my god," she said in a breathless rush, fanning her face. "I have to tell her. This is really bad. She could put someone in the hospital with this. Be right back."

Chad picked up a floret of cauliflower and dragged it through the dip, chuckling as Piper disappeared around the corner, her next cough speaking volumes.

While Piper and Joy went to work trying to rescue the punch Chad wandered into the living room. Dominic and another man were picking out music on an MP3 together.

His host turned. "You must be Chad," he said extending his hand. "I'm Dom and this is Trey."

Trey shook Chad's hand next. "You must have met Celia in the kitchen."

"I did." Chad said brightly. "So what's the plan?"

Back in the kitchen Piper took a second wary taste of punch and declared it good. She ladled two fresh glasses and brought one out to Chad.

Dom laughed. "I guess I should take the blame for the punch. I never drink the stuff so I just poured until it looked right. I didn't bother tasting it."

"It could have peeled paint," Joy said with pursed lips and gave him an elbow in the ribs. She turned to Chad and Piper. "Come on, I'll introduce you around some more."

Eventually their hosts moved on to circulate among the ever increasing number of guests, leaving Piper and Chad to mingle on their own. Piper felt just as out of place as Chad did, having brought the only other person she knew with her.

As more people arrived there was an effort to get a game of charades going but that idea fizzled and instead they moved the music out to the backyard and the patio was turned into a dance floor.

Chad looked at Piper. "Do you dance?"

"Not unless I've been drinking."

He laughed and took the glass out of her hand, setting it aside. "Good, we've met that condition."

"I mean I'm usually more than a little tipsy," she said, overly aware of his hand suddenly curled around her waist.

He turned her smoothly into his arms and they swayed, fingers fused, bodies pressed so close they could have buttoned their shirts together. Chad's aftershave was fading but Piper found that even more unsettling because now, this close, his natural scent was quietly emerging and mingling with the cologne. She liked it, a little too much. It was a powerful double whammy, smelling him, feeling him against her.

The tempo of the next song was more energetic so they separated to gyrate, bump, and spin laughing as they tried all the ridiculous moves they could remember.

"Not bad for a woman who doesn't dance," he teased, leading her off the pavers afterwards.

"I do my best." She looked around. "Where did I leave my glass?"

"I left it, remember?" He reached out to pick it up from the wooden table where he set it earlier and stopped. "Never mind. You don't want this one. There's a hornet in it."

They went back inside and filled two fresh glasses with punch. Piper tipped hers back and the world shifted on her. Feeling a little fuzzy in the head she grabbed the edge of the table to steady herself.

"Wow. Still has a kick," Piper said licking her lips and contemplating her empty glass. "I got a little dizzy when I tipped my head back. Maybe I need a straw." She turned and stared at the cabinets thoughtfully. "I wonder if Joy has any straws."

"Forget it. I think we should both probably switch to water."

"Party pooper," she said with a pout.

Chad put his hand on Piper's shoulder and turned her towards the table. "Eat something. Food might help."

"I'm not hungry."

"Eat." Chad held a strawberry against her lips until she opened her mouth. He smiled as he popped it in. "There. That wasn't so bad, was it?"

Piper rolled her eyes then blinked when it made her dizzy. "You don't have to take care of me. I'm not your daughter, you know."

"I hope not."

He pushed another large strawberry on her and after she swallowed it she slipped his empty cup inside hers and sashayed over to the garbage can. She stopped and stared at the heaping container, then set the glasses on the counter.

"I can't leave it like this. I wonder where Joy keeps fresh bags." She opened the obvious cabinets but came up empty handed.

"Maybe in here?" Chad tried a door off the kitchen and they found themselves in a small laundry room with utility cupboards. They scavenged but this was evidently not where she kept her trash bags either.

"Let's not worry about it," he said finally.

"I just wanted to help, that's all."

"I know. That's very sweet."

Because neither of them bothered to slide the doorstop into place, the laundry door had swung silently closed behind them leaving only a narrow two inch gap. Giving up the search with a sigh, Piper reached for the knob to pull it open.

Chad's hand shot out and caught hers, startling them both. Piper turned and looked at him in surprise and he moved closer, relenting to the temptation that had dogged him all evening.

She knew he was going to kiss her. She needed him to kiss her. She stumbled backwards into the door and it shut firmly behind her.

23

Piper looked up at him and smiled and Chad could see the spirits glittering in her eyes. She wasn't exactly sober and his impulse to kiss her wavered. Maybe now wasn't the best time to take advantage. But then, apparently sensing his hesitation, Piper lifted his hand to her lips and kissed his knuckles.

Chad held his breath and watched the soft brush of her lips make contact with his hand. He felt the moist teasing stroke of her tongue in the valley of his knuckles and groaned.

"What are we doing?" he said softly, stepping closer and running his free hand down her hair.

"Do you want to stop?" she asked, her lips softly sealing over his knuckle.

"Probably should." He stroked her cheek with the back of his fingers.

"That's not what I asked."

"I know."

He slid his hand behind her head and caught a handful of hair then gently yet firmly tugged her head back. Moving in, he pressed his body flush against hers and dipped down to kiss her. Piper moaned and rubbed him harder, purring as she ground over his erection. Their kiss deepened and soon Piper was clinging to him.

When Chad finally eased back to take a breath, she nuzzled at his throat and inhaled. "You smell so good tonight. You've been driving me crazy."

"Why do we torture ourselves like this?" Chad asked, nipping and licking down her neck.

"Insanity?" She ran her hands down his chest and found his nipples with her thumbs.

"I want you – so much."

"I want you, too."

Chad seized Piper, lifting her right off her feet. Her legs and arms wrapped tightly around him and he carried her over to the washer as they fed from each other. He set her down on top and put his finger to his lips. "We have to be quiet."

Piper nodded and flexed her fingers into his hair like a cat. Chad groaned and dipped his head to nuzzle between her breasts. When she didn't object or stop him he took it further, thrusting her shirt and bra up with one quick move to expose her tight nipples.

Piper's head fell back as he latched onto her breast and sucked her deep, his mouth, his tongue doing rhythmical things to her she wasn't strong enough to resist. It was sweet exquisite torture but it wasn't enough, not nearly enough, yet it still managed to get the machine rumbling like thunder beneath her.

She was running short of patience when she hauled his shirt out of his pants then leaned back, breaking his suction on her breast with a loud pop. Now she could tug his shirt over his head. Once he was bared, she needed a minute to simply admire him. He was a feast for the senses.

"I don't want to want you so much," she said, taking Chad's face in her hands and kissing him hard.

"Not my fault." He kissed her back.

"Where are you?" she demanded, working at his fly.

He tore his mouth away. "You're too high, anyway."

He set her on her feet and dragged her pants down. His were already pooled around his ankles and together they stepped free of their clothing. Chad kicked it aside.

"Now," she whispered into his ear then sucked his earlobe. "Who knows how much time we have?"

She slid to the floor and Chad stretched out over her. Her eyes were sparkling when she looked into his.

"This is the last time," she said quite seriously.

"Whatever you say," he agreed impatiently.

Her knees came up around him and he thrust deep. Piper sighed, running her hands all over him.

"I needed this," she admitted softly. "I really needed this. You feel so good."

"So do you," he said, kissing her.

Chad moved to thrust again but his cotton socks slid out across the vinyl floor behind him. He had no grip.

"Hold on," he grunted then grabbed Piper around the waist and hauled her back with him to the wall so he could brace his feet. With a sigh he took another shot at it but this time Piper slipped away from him.

"Shit! Did she just wax the fucking floor?" He swore in frustration. "Hold onto me—hard," he ordered.

For some odd reason Piper was completely turned on by the command. She wanted him, now, more than ever. She was his to possess and she hoped he did it soon. She grabbed hold of his shoulders and hooked her heels behind his knees and when he drove into her she quivered with unimagined relief.

"Don't go easy on me," she whispered in his ear then sucked his lobe.

Her breath, her words drove him crazy. "Don't tempt me," he growled. She laughed, low and rich. "Chad, nail me to the floor."

"Just remember that you asked for it."

After a week of sexual frustration and no release he took his foot off the brake and hit the accelerator. He didn't have to hold back or control the need to satisfy her again. He had her permission to let loose and he was willing to give her everything she asked for.

He teased her at first, with long slow drives that made her legs shake. She lifted her hips, almost frantic to swallow him faster, urge him along but he was in control and there wasn't anything she could do about it.

Then he changed again, dropping into her heavily, using the weight of his hips to add to the force of each deep thrust. Piper shuddered and gasped, shifting herself so that he would hit the spot that would allow her to take complete advantage of each jarring and delicious impact.

Right before his eyes Piper's face colored like the blushing sunset and Chad picked up the pace; stabbing into her harder and harder, faster and faster, hoping to keep up. Neither felt the tiny granules of sand they were grinding into their bare skin.

"Oh god, Chad," her voice wavered on the brink.

There was panic and pleasure swirling in her eyes and he knew from experience what she was warning. He grinned and shoved his thumb into her mouth, hoping it would help mute her orgasmic cries but she started sucking it, teasing it with her tongue and the sensations shot right through him. With a groan he went wild, pounding into her body like a tenderizing hammer and Piper's glow deepened. She strained desperately to absorb every crash until finally the collisions rebounded on them and their bodies seized, shattering them into particles and returning them to their truest forms.

Only after they recovered did they realize how lucky they were not to get caught in this unlocked room. They laughed like naughty kids while they dressed, coming together for one last lingering kiss and grope before cautiously opening the door and slipping into the empty kitchen.

They found Joy in the back yard and said their good-byes.

Walking back to Piper's car Chad asked, "Mind if I drive?"

"Why?"

"Because I'm more comfortable behind the wheel."

"Fine." She tossed the keys to him and smiled, impressed when he caught them in the dying light.

"Thanks."

"Welcome."

He gave her a meaningful look over the roof. "No—*thanks.*"

Now that the heated coupling was over she blushed bashfully as she smiled back. "Thank you, too."

"Last time." He didn't mean a word.

"Absolutely," she agreed.

He drove to his dark worksite and they parked like a couple of teenagers, steaming up the windows, consuming each other hungrily. Both looked like they'd been through a Chicago windstorm when they parted, a good deal later than expected and with the promise that this really would be the last time.

24

It was just after two in the afternoon and Piper and Joy were finishing their clean-up when Joy gave her a yell.

"Piper, someone's here to see you."

Piper put away the broom and dustpan.

As they passed, Joy whispered, "He's cute."

"Yeah." Piper agreed grudgingly. She stopped just back from the case and looked over the top with unfriendly eyes. "Mick."

He smiled back at her, ignoring her moods like he always had. "Hi ya, luscious."

"How did you find me?"

"I called your mom."

"She told you where I am?" Piper blustered furiously. "Nice to know who you can trust." She took a second to calm herself but her next question came out sharper than intended anyway. "Why did you want to know?"

He laughed, unfazed. "Still the best at farting out the candles, I see."

Her eyes narrowed.

"Come on Piper, chill out. I have something of yours and I know you're going to want it back. Are you about done here?"

"I can take care of the rest," Joy called out from the back.

Piper shook her head. "Yeah, I guess. Let me get my things."

Joy's curiosity was working overtime when she watched Piper punch out and grab her purse from her locker. For once she didn't bother changing out of her work shoes before walking out from behind the counter and leaving with Mick through the store instead of using the employee entrance.

Theirs was a silent walk broken only when she saw his car in the lot. "You're kidding. *That's* still running?"

"More or less."

They stopped at the back and she rolled her eyes at the "Ski Naked" bumper sticker curling up in two corners while he found his key. He slid it into the lock.

Turning to her Mick said, "So I'm moving to Colorado. Do you remember Ed?"

"Morino?"

"Yeah. He looked me up. He's gonna be running this new restaurant right off the slopes and he thought of me. He wants me for sous-chef. The money's good."

"Colorado?"

"Yeah. I should be able to get in a lot of skiing."

Among other things. "Sounds like your dream job."

He grinned. "I know. I'm really psyched about it."

"What'll you do in the warmer months?"

"I'll squeeze a little work in between the climbing, biking, and rafting. Work just enough to afford my beer and digs." He was jumpy with excitement.

"Think this old beast is going to make it?" She nudged the bumper with her knee.

"No way. Do you know anyone who might be interested in a twelve-year-old Volvo?"

Knowing how he took care of things she gave a hasty shake of the head.

"Actually I'm heading out with Saundra. He offered her something, too."

She remembered Saundra. Mick had enjoyed a few tumble sessions with that slut while they were still together. "Are you seeing her now?"

His expression soured. "No, we're just having fun. I expect we'll both be ready to move on when we get there and check out the new menu."

She'd heard enough. "You said you found something of mine?"

"Yeah." Mick finally turned the key and opened up the back. Reaching inside he slid a large box towards her.

"My grandmother's linens," Piper whispered, distressed that she never even missed them.

"This was in the cage in the basement. I didn't recognize the box when I was packing up so I almost sent it with a bunch of stuff to the Salvation Army."

She ran her hand over the box then looked at him. "Thanks for not doing that."

He shrugged. "When I opened it and saw what it was I knew you'd want it back so don't be too mad at your mom, okay?"

"I'm not anymore."

"I'll put this in your car for you. Where are you parked?"

She pointed at the far corner of the parking lot.

"I'm not walking it all the way over there. Get in, we'll drive it over."

He opened the passenger door for her and she had to chuck a handful of garbage over the seat and onto the floor before she could sit down. He closed her door and went to the other side.

When he got in she said, "Why don't you ever throw this crap away? It's so easy to do it when you gas up. Honestly, the garbage cans are right there, pretty hard to miss."

"Piper, I shouldn't need to remind you that you don't get to nag me anymore. Let it go."

She laughed at herself. "You're right."

And that's all it took, his simple reminder to let it go and she felt the weight of the past release her, too.

When Chad spotted Piper outside the store he searched for the closest parking space, before pulling into one the next aisle over. She wasn't expecting him this afternoon but he hoped he could entice her into spending a quiet evening with him. If kissing or, say, sex came into play, all the better. God, he couldn't get over how good it felt just looking at her.

He settled back, giving her time to finish her conversation but then she climbed into the other guy's car and Chad felt a crushing pain clamp down on his chest.

They were still talking when they backed out. Chad's agony increased tenfold when Piper laughed, her happiness unmistakable.

Chad took a deep breath and pounded the heel of his hand on the steering wheel several times while he cursed and swore at himself. Then he threw the car in reverse and shot out of the parking lot, wondering why the hell he never listened to her when she warned him off.

Mick found Piper's car without any help and stopped right behind it. It was the work of a moment to transfer the box from his car to hers and they parted, one last time with a sincere hug and good wishes between them.

Piper was unusually quiet when Mick drove off with a final wave. Lost in thought, she didn't hear Joy come up behind her.

"So what was that all about?"

Piper glanced over. "Mick's moving to Colorado and he found something of mine in storage. He just brought it to me."

"Seriously? That was unexpectedly nice of him."

Piper looked at her. "I never said Mick wasn't nice. He's as charming as a diplomat. That's why people like him and why I was vulnerable to a backslide but his Achilles' heel has always been self-interest. He'll do anything for you as long as it doesn't conflict with what he wants or inconvenience him too much."

"Are you still susceptible to his charm?"

A radiant smile broke across Piper's face and she shook her head. "I can finally say with absolute confidence that I'm really and truly free of him. It just took me longer than I thought it would to realize it." Her smile deepened. "Come on, I think we need to celebrate."

The girls popped back into the liquor store then caravanned to Joy's house where they polished off two pitchers of margaritas over the course of a few hours. Not a good idea on an empty stomach.

Already past the point of no return Joy stumbled to the refrigerator and yanked open the door. She stared stupidly as it crashed into the counter and sent the bottles in their tracks rattling together. Piper giggled and tripped up behind her. She caught hold of the door and pulled it back, studying the fresh dent in the metal without comment.

"Here." Joy handed a package of celery back to her.

"That's it?" Piper frowned. "You work in a grocery store for god's sake. Can't you shop once in a while?"

"Bite me." Joy rummaged some more and stood up. "Ah ha. We have a jar of olives, too." She slapped her hand against the freezer to steady herself.

"Olives and margaritas?"

"Why not. It's not like we're going to be able to taste anything anyway," Joy said with a pronounced slur.

"If that's all there is, the celery's mine."

Piper hugged it to her chest possessively and tripped over to the table. Dropping gracelessly onto a chair she pulled back the plastic sleeve and tore off a few stalks. Now, frowning at the rest she realized she could afford to share her bounty. Piper ripped a few more stalks free and set them on the table for Joy. The rest she tossed into the center of the table then picked up one of the stringy stalks with a scowl.

Turning to Joy hopefully she said, "Tell me you have peanut butter."

"It's salt-free."

"Salt-free? What is wrong with you?"

"Not me, Dom."

"What's wrong with him?"

"There's not enough time to go into it."

"My life's looking better and better."

Joy sat down and eyed the celery in front of her. After chewing unenthusiastically for a minute she sighed. "Maybe we should just order pizza and be done with it." She set her stalk down and reached for the olives. Fishing a couple out of the jar with her fingers she popped one into her mouth hoping to neutralize the taste of celery but shuddered in disgust instead.

"Ugh. I was wrong. I *can* taste it. Don't even go there. Olives clash with margaritas—big time."

"So we're ordering pizza?"

"Damn straight." Joy grabbed her phone.

While they waited for the delivery Joy decided it was time to pry. "I really liked Chad. What's happening there?"

Piper turned her head too fast and it felt like she was turning a boat on the water. She enjoyed the swimmy sensation for a second before answering. "I *really* like him, too." Then she giggled.

"Is that all?"

Piper gave her a naughty smile. "I jumped him in your laundry room Saturday."

"You did not!"

"What if I did, would you be mad at me?"

"No. At least you left my bed alone."

Piper's eyes widened. "You know something? We've never even *done it* in a bed."

"Seriously? Why not?"

"No idea." Piper drummed on the table with two celery stalks until the longer one broke.

Joy stared off, deep in thought.

Piper grinned at her. "Don't strain the brain over there."

Joy's eyes refocused. "I think I know."

"About the bed? You couldn't."

"Just hear me out."

172

"Like you're going to make any sense now." Piper snorted. "You're wasted."

"And you're not? Give me some credit. So here's my thought. Maybe, just maybe a bed represents a relationship to you. Don't shake your head at me. Listen. You have to admit, you've been pretty resistant to that thought."

"So now you're a therapist?"

Joy continued over Piper's interruption. "Just like Mick."

"What?" Piper exploded at the comparison.

"You said he was nice but emotionally detached."

Piper held up her hand. "I've heard enough."

"He wasn't a relationship kind of person."

"You're pissing me off."

"Didn't want people to expect things from him or rely on him."

"He acted like a spoiled child. He wasn't capable of going any deeper than sex." Piper glared at her.

"Sound like anyone you know?"

"You bitch."

"You said yourself that he wasn't exactly interested in growing up which forced you to be the adult. No wonder you resented it. You couldn't act the same way. Now you're alone and you have everything just the way you want it and you only have to think of yourself. It must make you very happy."

"You've completely misconstrued the situation."

"Have I? I'm not the one who said I'm reverting." She tried to take Piper's hand but she pulled it away. "Piper, I love you but sometimes you can be a charming, selfish woman."

"How can you say that?"

"Are you using Chad for sex?"

"No, I care about him. We're friends."

"But you keep sleeping with him."

"I can't help it."

"Liar."

173

Piper threw her celery at Joy, missing her. She was suddenly really uncomfortable about the parking she and Chad did after the party. It added weight to what Joy was saying and she didn't like it. There was no way Joy was going to hear about that now, too.

The doorbell rang.

"Since you seem to think that everyone just wants to use you anyway you might as well pay for the pizza. Add me to the list," said Joy irritably.

Piper stomped drunkenly across the carpet and pulled money out of her purse. When she came back with the pizza box she intended to throw it down on the table but she was so unsteady she missed. Joy managed to catch it before it plunged off the edge of the table. She slid it safely into the middle.

"Here." She shoved a plate at Piper and they served themselves.

Emotions were high as they chewed, their tempers festering at first then collapsing before they finished their first slices. As if on cue they both started crying at the same time and dropped their crusts, leaning in to hug each other.

"I'm sorry," Joy said, swiping at her tears.

"No, I'm sorry. Do you really think I'm acting like Mick?" Piper blubbered.

"I only have your description of him to go on, but yeah." Joy nodded apologetically.

"But I'm not emotionally closed off." Piper blew her nose into her napkin.

Joy giggled. "Right now, I can see that."

Piper laughed and they hugged again.

"I think we're done with these," Joy said, picking up their glasses and carrying them to the sink. She dumped them both down the drain. "We're switching to water."

They fell asleep in front of the television, a romantic comedy playing on without an audience. Piper's telephone vibrated softly in her purse, sending yet another call into voicemail.

25

After Chad sped off in his car Sunday afternoon, he drove around brooding silently, and sometimes not so silently, for over an hour until he trusted himself enough to call Piper. Of course when she didn't pick up he was back to the beginning again. The message he left her was brief. It had to be. For the rest of the night he waited expectantly for a call back. Once he even made sure his phone was on and had power just in case that was the reason it wasn't ringing. When his last two attempts to reach her sent him directly into her voicemail he gave up in frustration.

Chad was glum when he put the kids to bed. He picked up a book and took it to his room, hoping like hell it would distract him from the reality of his crumbling romantic aspirations but the words flowed together before his eyes, indecipherable.

Friends. Piper said she just wanted to be friends, but he was confused. How many friends fucked like animals and then went back to being casual with each other? Was he the only one with actual feelings involved here? He didn't think so.

No, he decided more firmly. There was definite, unmistakable tension between them and no matter how much Piper protested that she didn't want to be involved, they were. Why the hell didn't she realize it? But then he thought, maybe *his* emotions were clouding his judgment. It wasn't entirely impossible to imagine that he'd projected what he wanted to see onto her.

He'd never felt so confused in his life.

The worst thoughts hit him shortly after midnight. That's when he started to wonder how many other *friends* she had. He hated how his mind strayed in that direction but he was becoming unhappily aware that he probably wasn't the only one. He saw enough yesterday to draw some pretty uncomfortable conclusions.

Did he have any right to feel jealous or possessive? Damn it, no, but he didn't screw around casually either and as a single parent, he owed it to his kids to be cautious about sexual and emotional entanglements because whatever he did could potentially impact them, too. If he wasn't Piper's exclusive stud he had a right, an obligation even, to know.

By twelve-thirty he arrived at the moment of truth for whatever this was between them. He decided to lay everything out once and for all and find out whether there was any reason to keep trying or if it was time to cut Piper out of his life entirely. He knew in his own heart that for him, it was all or nothing. He wouldn't hover on the periphery of her life hoping that she might throw him the occasional bone with the possibility of more to come in the indistinct future. No, he was certain about one thing at least, he couldn't go on loving a woman who refused to love him back. His future hinged on what Piper said when she returned his call tomorrow and if she had any compassion at all, she'd make it early.

Piper woke up Monday morning with the most painful headache imaginable. It hurt just to open her eyes and brought on an alarming nausea. She staggered into Joy's guest bathroom and vomited, crying silently the entire time because retching made the pounding even more excruciating.

Joy must have gone up to bed sometime during the night. Since it was their day off, Piper didn't want to wake her just to tell her she was going home. She penned a quick note and slipped out, driving home to sleep off the effects of the alcohol and do something about her headache.

Chad got good news early Monday. With all the barrels recovered, they were almost ready for the last of the excavation to proceed but there were still soil samples at the lab and while not all the results were in yet, what he'd learned so far was promising. They didn't have to worry that they were sitting on a super-fund site anymore. In the meantime, everything else was on track. The trenches for the foundation were completed and the steel rebar was bent and shaped to strengthen the concrete.

Chad signed papers on the top of his car and handed them off. "I'll be at my office if you need to reach me," he told the man.

He was haggard when he got into his car and even though he knew it was pointless, Chad tried Piper's phone for the second time that morning. It sent him straight to voicemail. He was beyond rage when he snapped his phone shut and swore.

Why did he even give a shit? Duh, the *why* was obvious. All he could do now was make sure he gave her a chance to explain before he made his final decision.

As the hours wore on and Piper still refused to call, Chad grew more resigned, then calloused, finally accepting her terms of their relationship for the first time. He was at the all-or-nothing point and it looked like the decision had already been made for him. He was just pathetically slow to realize he'd just gotten the kiss-off.

The last irrefutable nail in his relationship coffin came when Piper didn't show up for his game that night. Chad didn't know why he still watched for her, why he still hoped to see her but as far as Chad's team was concerned his distraction made him completely useless. After the game, he broke precedent and went out with a few of his teammates to drown their sorrows. Defeat was hard enough but after a trouncing like that everyone felt like wallowing. Chad was among friends.

Piper tried calling Chad on Tuesday but she couldn't get through. She didn't know why he wasn't picking up but finally, after a long wait, she was able to leave him a message.

"Hi Chad it's Piper. I'm really sorry I didn't get back to you sooner but I hung out with Joy on Sunday and ended up crashing at her place then yesterday I felt so lousy I could hardly get out of bed. Call me."

Chad waited until he got home to listen to her message. It wasn't something he relished doing. By the time he deleted it and closed his phone he was livid. The lying bitch! He saw who she left with on Sunday and that wasn't Joy. Then, then to have the nerve to tell him she spent the next day in bed was unbelievably low. Of course the slut stayed in bed. That guy probably didn't have kids to storm in and bust them at any moment. And as far as being sick went, well, she looked pretty damned healthy on Sunday.

He tried hard to remember her reasons, in detail, for not wanting to get involved with anyone. Resentment had been a big part of it. She said straight out that she resented Mick for making her take responsibility for both of them. She only wanted to be responsible for herself now.

Chad slapped himself in the forehead. He was so stupid. She'd been warning him. She told him she wasn't interested in dating or becoming a part of his family package and still he pushed, hoping that their chemistry would overrule her stubbornness. That hope had blown right up in his face. How does it feel now, slick?

"Missy!" Chad bellowed. "Come on, we have to get going!"

She clomped down the steps, her little sandals slapping the bottoms of her feet. He noticed her painted toenails and wondered who gave her the polish.

"Do you have your present?" he snapped.

She nodded, pulling back uneasily.

He didn't notice. "Fine. Get in the car."

Piper's phone rang and she answered it right away. "Chad?"

"No, it's Joy."

"Oh, hi."

"How're you feeling?"

"Better. You?"

"I thought I was going to die yesterday."

Piper laughed. "Me too."

"What's going on?"

"Nothing apparently."

"You want to hang out? Dom is stuck working late."

"No booze."

"Deal."

Following Missy into the party room, Chad recoiled at the noise. He wasn't up to handling a bunch of squirrelly little girls. Then he saw Angela Markland heading over with that predatory smile of hers locked on him and he knew the little girls were the least of his worries.

Angela put an extra little bounce in her step so her ample breasts jiggled for him. The woman had cleavage to spare and she was eager to share.

"Chad," she said reaching for his arm when he didn't lean down for a peck on the cheek. "Thanks for coming early, you're a doll. Apparently no one watches the time anymore. I didn't expect so many girls to get dropped off already. I'm not even set up yet."

She tucked Chad's arm through hers and led him inside, sidestepping running children as they walked Missy's present over to the gift table.

"What is it you want me to do?" he asked.

She gave him a slow feline smile.

"Let's just start with games for now. We'll be playing musical chairs over there, clothespins in a jar, and I have a pin the tail on the donkey game that needs to be set up on that peg board. Take your pick."

"How many kids are coming to this?"

"I expect twenty girls."

He tried not to shudder. "Fine. Why don't I start with the donkey poster?"

"Not too high."

No shit. "Are there any tacks?"

"Over there." She pointed to a table along the wall with several brown paper bags standing on it.

Chad didn't even want to think about how many times he felt her hungry eyes following him as he worked. Once while he was moving tables out of the way to make room for musical chairs he nearly jumped out of his skin at the look on her face. He honestly thought she was going to pounce. He was stressed enough as it is, he really didn't need this right now.

Angela was the *Sex and the City* mom: divorced, active, and on the prowl. For two years she'd eyed him like a Popsicle but he was friends with her ex-husband and he knew too many things about her to consider it. One faithless woman screwing with his life was enough.

Angela finished decorating the birthday girl's chair like a throne then showed Chad where she wanted the plates and napkins set up. While he did that she called everyone together and started them on pin the tail on the donkey in the corner.

Assuming that his work was finally done, Chad sat down and zoned out, trying to clear his mind of every painful thought but his eyes shot open when the girls let out a piercing racket.

He wanted to flee when he heard Angela say, "Go see the prize papa."

He looked at her with a question, his hands in the air.

"Give her a gift," she said, pointing.

"What?" He sat up.

"They're in the bags over there. Any one will do."

He led the girl over to the prize table and let her reach in herself. When she skipped off he thought he might as well plant himself there but Angela called him back.

"Chad, would you mind playing the music for musical chairs?"

"Why not?" Could this party get any worse?

Angela had an old-fashioned record player and small seventy-eights, the songs so lame he wanted to grind his teeth. He set the first record spinning and turned away from the action so that he could stay impartial. After all, his daughter was playing, too.

Slowly, chairs crowded around him until they were finally down to one still in play. One of the contestants happened to be Cassidy, the birthday girl, and when she won, an ugly battle broke out between Angela and her daughter over letting the other girl have the prize because Cassidy was already walking home with all the presents. It wasn't a pleasant situation and for a while it wasn't clear who was sulking more, Cassidy or Chad.

Angela sent Chad on a drink-finding mission while they played the clothespin game. He returned to the party room with a tray of Cokes and little enthusiasm. He set a glass at each place setting.

When the last game was finished Angela brought out the prize bag and invited any girl who hadn't already won something to come up and pull a prize. At least she had the foresight to bring enough for all the girls. Missy's arm was buried to her armpit when Chad went back out to the counter to wait for their pizzas.

He was standing off to the side when Piper and Joy walked in.

26

"Hey!" Piper broke into a happy smile. "I've been trying to reach you."

"I've been busy," Chad said coolly, hardly looking at her.

Chad in a bad mood was something new and it unnerved her. She frowned. "Didn't you get my message?"

"Yes," he snapped. "Didn't you get mine?"

Piper glanced at Joy, clearly bewildered. "I don't understand. I told you I was sick yesterday. By the time I woke up it was too late to call."

"Markland?" the man behind the counter called out.

"Here." Chad waved his hand and walked away from Piper without another word. He picked up the pizza. A second slid beside it. "Two?"

The man nodded.

"Fine. I'll be right back."

He strode off with the pizza, leaving Piper and Joy completely puzzled.

"What's with him?" Joy whispered.

"I don't know." Fear and icy dread were wringing out her insides.

"I'll get our sandwiches," said Joy.

"Thanks."

Joy walked away leaving Piper alone. When Chad came back out the glare he gave her was so sharp Piper nearly fell back.

Knowing it was all show Piper walked courageously over to him and said hotly, "Are you going to tell me what's wrong?"

He laughed; a bitter, unpleasant laugh. "I can't talk about it right now. It's not a good time."

"You're starting to scare me," she said softly, her anxiety

multiplying by the second.

A piranha in open-toed heels walked up behind him and curled her manicured fingernails over his shoulder possessively. "Chad, aren't you coming?"

Piper's blood chilled and the women faced off like rivals.

"Angela, this is Piper," Chad said. "She's just a friend."

His emphasis on the word *just* stung. They were more than that.

Angela's cold sneer spread into an insincere smile. "Any friend of Chad's…" She let the rest trail off and slipped her hand through his arm. "I could really use you in there."

"I'll be right with you. Could you grab the other pizza?" he asked.

"Sure. Don't be long," she said intimately, throwing Piper a dismissive look before sashaying off with the second pan.

"What's going on?" Piper demanded angrily. Tears were welling in her eyes and her heart was constricting in agony but she refused to back down now. He owed her an explanation, damn it.

Chad glared back at her, boiling with rage. "Don't you dare Piper!" he growled. "Don't you fucking dare! We've been playing by *your* rules all along. So now that I've wised up and realized that you actually meant them you have nothing to say about me being here with Angela. If I want to take out another woman I'm damned well going to because you made it perfectly clear that I wasn't taking you out."

Piper was shocked by his venom, stunned by his vulgar language, and rendered speechless by his argument. "Chad," she said, trying desperately to hold onto her composure, "I don't know what's going on here but this is not how friends treat each other."

He snorted. "Yeah, like you know how a friend behaves. You treat me like a fucking sex toy when the mood hits but you won't open yourself up in any other way."

Piper recoiled as if he'd struck her.

"I'm sorry," he continued, "but I can't play that way. I won't. We don't have a friendship. I don't even know what you'd call this but it doesn't resemble any friendship I've ever heard of."

A manager came up and in an urgent whisper, asked them to please take their argument outside.

"We're done here," Chad told him.

"No!" Piper burst out.

"We're done," he repeated firmly. "You created this mess so don't act like I've hurt *your* feelings. You got everything you wanted out of me. I don't think you should call me again."

"You pursued me," she reminded him helplessly.

He shook his head and finally smiled. It wasn't reassuring. "You're right. I should have left you alone when you asked. I'm sorry I didn't listen."

Angela poked her head around the corner. "Chad, are you coming?"

He gave her a quick nod and walked off.

If anything, his smile disturbed Piper even more than his temper. There was a finality to it that chilled her.

"I'm going to be sick," Piper said when Joy came back with their dinner in a bag.

"No shit." Joy took Piper by the arm and dragged her out; shaken, raw, and utterly devastated.

"Dom, I'm going to stay with Piper for a while. She's not doing so hot." Joy hung up the phone. "Okay, that's mine taken care of now let's work on your relationship."

"I don't have one."

"You did. What happened?"

"I wish I knew."

"I thought the mixed signals were a bad idea."

Piper glared at her with red puffy eyes. "He seduced me!"

Joy gave her a speculative look. "Whether he did or didn't doesn't matter. You kept going back to the candy dish for more even though you'd put yourself on a diet."

"You don't know anything about this."

"I know enough to see that you blew it."

Piper screamed into her pillow and kicked her legs.

"Feel better?" Joy asked.

"No."

"So what do you want from him?"

"Everything," Piper whispered.

Joy broke into an ecstatic smile. "I knew it! You love him!"

"Why can't we decide when we want to fall in love?"

Joy ruffled Piper's hair. "It wouldn't be called falling then. You can't choose when the right guy is going to come along but when he does, it's your responsibility to recognize him. You chose to fight it instead, confusing yourself and Chad in the process. Not something I would've done. Maybe he's just had enough."

"I'm so confused. I never expected anything like this. I didn't know he could get so mad."

"I, I, I, I." Joy frowned. "Do you hear yourself? I have to remind you of something here. Do you remember how you described your perfect guy?"

"When?"

"When I asked you to go on a blind date with Dom's friend."

"Vaguely."

"I remember. You said he had to be employed, considerate, responsible, and mature. You also wanted both sides of Santa's list."

"What?"

Joy smiled. "That's how I remembered it. You said he should be naughty and nice."

"God, that's right. Did you tape that conversation or something?"

"No, I just paid attention for future reference. I thought if I kept my eyes open I might be able to find you a guy that fit it. But you found him first, all by yourself. What amazes me is that you still don't believe it."

"As I recall, I said I wasn't looking." Piper rolled onto her back and stared at the ceiling.

"Honey, love doesn't work that way."

"If he'd just been patient until I was ready..."

"Did you ever wonder if maybe he isn't confused about *his* feelings? What if, deep down, he knows yours even better than you do? Did you ever talk about it? And as far as patience is concerned, need I remind you that he's been alone for years? Just how much patience do you expect him to have?"

"I just didn't want to hurt him."

"That worked out, didn't it?"

"What do you mean?"

"What else would make a man so angry?"

"You think he's in love with me and I hurt him somehow?"

Joy nodded. "I'd lay money on it."

"What should I do? Chad doesn't want to see me again. He told me not to call him."

Joy shook her head. "He wants to hear from you. Maybe not right now, but believe me, he's going to be looking for an explanation."

"Good, so am I. I want to know what just happened."

Angela's proposition came while they were loading the birthday presents into her trunk. She was nothing if not predictable.

Angela placed her hand on Chad's arm and said, "Looks like you could use a little grown-up company about now. What do you say? My bar is fully stocked. You're a Beefeater's man, as I recall."

"Not for a long time." Chad stepped back and her hand fell away. "Angela, I appreciate the invitation but I'm not up to it. I have a splitting headache."

She considered him quietly and finally accepted his excuse. "Chad, we're old friends, right?"

Chad nodded. Outright denial would be rude.

"Then talk to me. Get it off your chest." Her eyes strayed to his chest for a weighted moment. "I guarantee you'll feel better. I'd be happy to help with whatever it is that's upsetting you."

Reading her true objective wasn't hard. Chad gave it ten minutes, tops, before she turned her sympathy into a sexual advance. Her transparency made his skin crawl. He'd had enough of friends like that. Besides, she wasn't above using any advantage to slash at Piper in order to win his confidence and move into the vacancy she could smell like blood in the water. Even he could see, as pissed off as he was, that wouldn't be fair to Piper. If there was going to be a cat fight they should at least do it face to face, in the open, and let him get the hell out of their way.

On the way home, Chad stopped to pick up Kenny from his friend's house. Missy was still wired when he sent her up to bed but she went willingly enough. She could see her dad wasn't in the best mood again.

Kenny caught Chad in his bathroom swallowing a few tablets.

"Headache?" the boy asked.

"Yeah." Chad shut off the tap and grabbed a hand towel, pressing it to his face.

"Can I have ice cream?"

"Now?"

"I didn't get to go to the party."

Chad tossed the towel onto the counter and rubbed his eyes hard with his fingertips. "Okay," he said with a heavy sigh.

He followed the kid down the stairs, asking him once along the way to please walk a little quieter. They went into the kitchen and Chad scooped him up a bowl.

"Ben's mom and dad are getting a divorce," Ken said in between spoonfuls.

"I'm sorry to hear that. How's he taking it?"

"He's mad at them."

Chad nodded.

"Dad, if Mom didn't die, do you think you would have gotten divorced?"

Chad stared at his son, taken aback by the question. "It's hard to say," he finally answered. "We were happy, very happy, but I just don't know. Things can change. I hope we would have stayed together. I would have worked really hard to make it work."

"That's what I thought," Kenny said with a smile of relief. Chad ruffled his hair. "Hurry up, it's time for bed."

Kenny's question and confidence plagued Chad for the next few days. Would he have given up on Chelsea so quickly? If he really cared about Piper, and there was no denying that he did, didn't he owe her the opportunity to come clean? He'd been so shattered, so sure she played him false that he wasn't even open to listening when they unexpectedly ran into each other. No, he yelled, bullied, and swore at her. The memory shamed him. Then he issued a warning to stay away from him for Christ's sake, even though he picked up on her confusion right away. But he stamped out those niggling doubts and bludgeoned on.

He could still see Piper's happy smile when she saw him, the sheer pleasure alight in her eyes then the slow and painful pull of gravity as the muscles released, going slack so that her lovely smile vanished into a shocked "oh." She'd transformed right before his eyes. *He* did that to her.

Piper may have hurt him first but he retaliated in a cruel and very personal way. His was a vicious frontal assault, no ambiguity, no passive-aggressive bullshit. Now, he couldn't get her eyes out of his head, or forget her pain and confusion. They haunted him more because he'd made her cry.

By Friday Chad finally broke down and called her. He was glad that he had to leave a message. It was easier.

27

Piper expected his call, Joy guaranteed she'd get one, but she was afraid and not sure she wanted to take it. She hoped she'd get his voicemail, too, but unfortunately Chad picked up right away.

"Piper? Thanks for calling back."

"What do you need, Chad?" Her voice was flat, weary.

"I think we need to clear the air. Would you meet with me?"

She waited a beat before saying, "Where?" Piper heard his sigh of relief.

"I don't care. I can call my mom and have her take the kids tonight if you want to come over to my place."

"So you can have the home field advantage?"

"That's not why I suggested it. I'll come over to your place if that would make you feel more comfortable."

"No. I'll come by. What time?"

"When are you through with work?"

"I have an hour left."

"Good. I can knock off early, too. Let me call my mom and see if she can take the kids. I'll call you back as soon as I know."

Joy cheered when Piper cancelled on her.

"That's okay. We'll go windsurfing another time. But seriously, you're going over there? Do you want a referee?"

Piper shook her head. "I'll be fine."

"I saw how pissed he was at you. I'd be nervous."

"He would only hurt me emotionally."

"But that's just as bad."

Piper gave her an anxious smile. "I know."

A number of emotions hit Chad in succession when he opened the door to Piper; annoyance, disappointment, helplessness. Why couldn't one of them be positive? It hurt so much to drink her in and yet he needed that painful swallow to soothe his raw throat even though it burned going down. He blamed her for the pain. He blamed himself even more because he gambled and lost when he didn't take her warnings seriously.

"Hi. Come in."

"Back up first," Piper said, spearing him with a wary eye.

She waited for Chad to move back from the door before she ventured inside. He shut out the daylight behind her.

"Why don't we go back to the kitchen?" Chad suggested.

"So you can be closer to the knives?" The acid comment felt good. Even if it wasn't the best thing she could do right now she was in the mood to provoke him.

"Funny." He was already familiar, thanks Mom, to that kind of sarcasm.

She followed him back and took her usual stool. When she looked settled he asked, "Something to drink?" He pointed to a bottle of wine on the counter.

"I'd prefer water."

"Coming up."

So, Piper wasn't going to make this easy. But then, he supposed coming here wasn't easy either. She was probably waiting for the next shoe to drop. Could he blame her?

Piper took only a quick sip then held her glass in front of her with both hands, ready to raise it like a shield or fling it if necessary. She faced him with a somber expression.

Chad took a deep breath. "I suppose you know why I asked you over."

"I'm not into guessing games."

He sighed. "I thought I should hear you out. Give you a chance to explain yourself."

"Me!" she burst out. "If anyone's owed an explanation I think it's pretty clear you owe me one, along with a big juicy apology."

Chad's mouth fell open. Oh, this was rich!

"How can you sit there and play innocent?" he asked in disgust.

"If I'm guilty of something it's customary, at least in this country, to let the accused know the charges against them. What is it exactly that I did? I'm a little confused here."

Chad struggled to control his temper but he was royally pissed now. "I *saw* you." He turned to the window and hit the counter with his open hand making the sugar dish jump and clatter. "I drove to Klein's on Sunday to invite you out to dinner and there you were, all friendly with some other guy in the parking lot."

When she merely stared at him with raised eyebrows and an expectant expression he pointed an accusing finger at her. "You got into his car, damn it! Then," he waved a crazy hand at the ceiling, "you completely blew off my phone calls. What was I supposed to think?" Suddenly Chad went into an amusing imitation of Piper's voice. "'Oh, and yesterday I didn't feel good so I stayed in bed all day.'"

Piper's lips twitched, as if she knew something he didn't. Chad was not amused.

"First of all," Piper broke in. "I wasn't expecting to see you after work so you can hardly blame me for making other plans and second of all, I wasn't aware I needed to get your approval in advance for every conversation I have. You're acting pretty possessive for a *friend*."

He opened and closed his mouth a few times, his mind scurrying to find an explanation. Before he could offer anything she went on.

"For your information, I *was* with Joy on Sunday night but since you brought him up, that was Mick. He dropped by the store at the end of my shift with something of mine that I left in his storage locker. You see, he's moving out of state and he thought I might like my grandmother's linens back. He offered to put them in my car but since he didn't know where I was parked when he pulled in, we had to drive over to it. Do you need to see the box or have a notarized statement from Mick in order to believe me? How about confirmation of his first and last months' deposit on his new apartment in Colorado? Would that make you feel more secure?"

The painful bands around Chad's chest released their grip only to be replaced by horror at how he acted, what he thought for the past week. How could he even begin to explain?

"Why didn't you call me Monday?" he asked quietly.

"I already told you, I was sick. I went over to Joy's and we had a margarita night and the next morning I had the mother of all hangovers. It was the worst I've ever had by the way, and I didn't feel up to making phone calls while I was hanging over the toilet with red tile marks cut into my bare knees."

Chad felt terrible. Just remembering the venom of his attack on her, his very public and evidently unfair attack, was distressing. "Really?"

"Really." She took this opportunity to ask, "Who the hell is Angela?"

There was a subtle twitch at the corner of his mouth when he thought about this comedy of errors they'd fallen into.

"She's Cassidy's mom. Cassidy is Missy's best friend. I was helping out at her birthday party."

Piper scowled at him. "You tried to make me think there was something going on there."

"Maybe." He shrugged, then thought screw it. It was time for complete honesty here. "Yes, I did."

"But you didn't sleep with her?"

"Never. Would you care?"

Her eyes said it all. "About as much as you'd care if I saw other guys."

That was a good answer. Chad smiled and walked around the counter. He lifted Piper's glass out of her hands and wrapped his arms around her, pulling her close.

Chad laid his cheek on the top of her head and sighed. "I'm sorry, so sorry. I was an ass."

Piper could finally admit to herself just how much she yearned for the smell of him, the feel of him but she needed to say this first. "I don't know if I'm ready to forgive you yet. You hurt me. You humiliated me. I'll never be able to show my face in Bruno's again."

He rubbed her back and laughed softly. "I admit I wasn't at my most rational right then and I suspect we're both probably banned from Bruno's now."

Piper's arms finally came up around Chad and it made them both feel better. "I thought you'd gone insane. You were using Angela to hurt me but I didn't understand why."

"I was. At least, I was trying to."

"Well, it worked."

"I'm sorry. As far as I was concerned, you hurt me first so I wanted to hurt you back. It was a reflex but believe me I was never interested in Angela."

"And I'm not interested in Mick."

Chad drew back to smile at her. "You say he's moving out of state?"

"Yes, but you were safe even when I hugged him goodbye."

"Are you saying what I think you're saying?"

Piper nodded. "I don't want to be your friend anymore."

"Don't toy with me. I've had a pretty lousy week."

"Welcome to the club." Piper snuggled against his chest. "Are we done being childish? Because I've gotta tell ya, at my age, I'm not up to it."

"God, yes."

Piper pulled back and looked at him. "Are you in love with me?"

He tipped his head and raised his eyebrows. "Do you love me?"

"I asked you first."

"This is straying back to childish again."

"Then answer the question."

He kissed the tip of her nose. "What do you think?"

"I think I was blind and stupid."

"Pretty hard to argue with that."

"Stop it," she warned.

"So what about you?"

"Do you remember when I told you that I wasn't going to fall in love with you?"

"Sounds vaguely familiar."

She smiled. "I was wrong. And then I was just too stubborn to admit it."

Chad's fingers combed through her hair and he tilted her head back so he could get at her mouth. When they finally came up for air, Chad rocked his forehead against hers and said, "I've been waiting for you to say that."

"That I was wrong?"

"No wonder my mom likes you. You've got the same exasperating sense of humor."

Piper laughed. "Chad?"

"Hmm?" he murmured as he kissed her temple.

"Will you take me to your bed?"

His answer was a soft kiss, a gentle smile, and a hand linking with hers to lead her upstairs.

28

This time, they approached each other thoughtfully, emotionally and physically bare. Instead of a manic need, a furious force inside them that demanded that each dominate and vie for control, there was tenderness, sharing, and giving.

When they stopped at the empty mirrored dresser, Piper smiled at Chad's reflection in the glass then turned Kenny's and Missy's photos face down. What was about to happen here was not for children's eyes.

Chad stepped up behind Piper and wrapped his arms around her waist, swaying back and forth in front of the mirror, his chin resting on her shoulder. Piper thought she could be content like this forever, at least until he moved up to the buttons on her shirt and released them, one by one. He drew the sides apart and with a flick, popped the front clasp holding her bra together. It sprang back and her breasts tumbled out but his hands were there to catch them. Piper sagged against his chest as he molded her, kneaded her. She shivered when he kissed the crook of her neck.

Then Chad took her hands in his and placed them over her breasts. They kneaded together for a minute before he moved off to skim down her stomach to the front of her jeans.

"Don't stop," he said, nipping at her neck when her hands stilled. She squeezed her breasts again and he smiled. "Good girl."

Chad tugged at her fly and Piper reached out to help him with the button but he shook his head and placed her hand back over her breast.

"Indulge me," he whispered, his warm breath a caress across her ear.

She cupped herself and he sighed, parting her zipper and drawing her pants down her legs. He paused to press a kiss to the small of her back then her panties slid down next, pooling around her feet.

Chad stood back up, his arm coming around her again and in one swift move he lifted her out of her clothing and spun her around, leaving them behind.

"That was the sexiest thing ever," she told him with a gasp.

He grinned. "I beg to differ."

Their hearts were pounding when he turned her back around so they both faced the mirror together. His eyes brushed over her naked body with long loving strokes. The waiting had been torture, the denial of their feelings ridiculous.

The intimate look in his eyes was her undoing. Piper never wanted anyone more in her life. Only Chad filled her in every possible way; her heart, her head, her dreams, her body. She needed to see him, touch him, taste him, and love him.

She twirled around and they attacked his clothing together, the need to press bare skin to bare skin almost unbearable. Still, Piper's eyes glittered when she finally got to look at him again. He was glorious; rough and smooth, warm and solid, strong yet gentle. There were so many ways she wanted to appreciate him, show him how much she desired him—how much she truly loved him. Oh god, she loved him so much.

"But I didn't want to love you," she confessed, one hand flowing over his hard hip, the other straying into his chest hair.

He smiled, running the back of his fingers along her cheek. "Sometimes we don't get what we want."

"But then we do." She smiled.

He tipped her face up and made her look him in the eye. "Are you sorry?" There was uncertainty in his voice.

"No." Piper pulled his head down so she could kiss him.

Then tears started leaking from the corners of her eyes and she tried to blink them away. "I was so afraid that you hated me on Tuesday." The memory made her shudder.

"Shh," he whispered, wrapping her in his arms and kissing her eyes. He could taste the salt on his lips. "I don't think we should go there again, okay?"

"Okay." She nodded and looked at the bed. "This is a big step for me."

"Me too. I've never shared this bed with anyone before."

She was shocked. "No one? Not even Chelsea?"

"I sold our old set. I couldn't look at it." He crouched down so he could look Piper in the eye. "I've never had a woman over because of the kids. You're the first."

The last of her doubts evaporated and she leaped into his arms, knocking him back onto the mattress, kissing him so hard he started laughing.

Chad turned his head away as she chewed and nibbled along his jaw. "I have a condition, Piper."

"What?" She ground her bottom over him suggestively.

"You stay the night—the whole night."

She stilled. "But I get up so early."

"How early?"

"Four."

"Four?"

"What can I say? I work in a bakery."

"Ugh," he groaned. "I have an alarm clock. We'll just need to re-set the coffeemaker to go off at the right time, too."

"So you still want me to stay?"

"I insist."

"But what about clothes?"

"There's an empty dresser over there, never used. I think I bought it for you three years ago. We should bring your stuff over as soon as we can."

"And what about the kids?"

"What about them?"

"I'm just surprised, that's all. What kind of example would we be setting? You're asking me to move in when you have kids to consider? Are you sure about that?"

"Hell yes. Besides, they know how I feel about you."

"They do? Was I the only one in denial?"

He threw his head back and laughed, heartily. "Apparently. I've been getting some serious counseling from both of them."

She smiled. "They kept your secrets."

He chucked her under the chin. "That's good to know, but you've raised the bigger subject."

"Which is?"

He tipped his head in a totally disarming, even charming way and smiled. "I know you could argue that we never officially dated though I'd argue back that as far as everyone else is concerned—me included—we've been paired up for some time."

"And your point is?"

"Piper, sweetheart, I've wanted you since the first time I saw you. I fell in love with you at the carnival."

"You did?"

He nodded and ran his fingers lightly up and down her bare arms. "I knew then where I wanted to go, where I wanted to take you, I've just been treading water, waiting for you to catch up. My next question might seem premature and if it is, I'll hold it steady as long as it takes but I'm hoping you won't make me wait too long. Piper, would you consider handcuffing yourself to me? Joining our family?"

Her heart jittered and twitched just hearing it. "Is this a proposal?"

"I know. It's not exactly how I planned it, either. I wanted to do this properly." He laughed for a minute, shaking beneath her. "But there was never any doubt in my mind that I'd be asking you to marry me eventually. The only thing I didn't know was when and where." His grin deepened, the deep cuts around his smile sharpened when he looked at their naked bodies pressed together.

"So I'm asking you now. I may not be dressed for the occasion and obviously I don't have a ring on me yet though you're welcome to do a body search if you like," he winked, "but if you want me to, I'll drop to my knee and ask the old fashioned way."

Piper simply stared at him, silent and surprised, and he panicked. "Oh shit, I've fucked up, haven't I?" He started stroking her arms, her sides anxiously, trying to soothe away her fears. "Piper, I'm so sorry. I'm rushing you. God, you just faced your feelings and here I am, pressuring you into a lifelong commitment. What the hell am I doing?"

Piper's smile was slow and amused. "As intriguing as the thought of you going down on one knee is, given your present state, the gesture isn't necessary." Then her voice broke. "Coming back to you here is like coming home from camp." Now Piper's tears ran in earnest.

Chad caught her hand, stopping her from wiping them away. The tenderness in his eyes was overwhelming. He pulled her down against him and kissed her salty cheek as Piper shook helplessly in his arms.

"You're afraid." He sought her eyes and she nodded. "I can wait if that's what you need."

Could her heart take any more? Piper doubted it. She caught his face in her hands and shook her head. "No. I love you Chad, more than I've ever loved anyone. You're my wish list, word for word, letter for letter. There's no need to wait because I want to wear your ring."

"Honestly?"

She nodded and his laughter lifted her heart like nothing else could.

He hugged her again, planting a kiss on her forehead. "Can we do this fast?"

"How fast?"

"I don't know. As soon as the license comes through. I want you home with me, with us. Any problems with that?"

She shook her head and smiled but he could see that there were things running through her mind and a new wave of doubts rolled over him.

"Hang on. I shouldn't hustle you into a quick wedding. You haven't had your special day yet. I'll bet you've been planning your wedding for years."

"I've had a number of them planned and the thing is they always change; from time of year, indoors or outdoors, who'll be in them, even what type of dress I'll wear. What hasn't changed is how I always wanted to feel about the man I made my promise to. I'm getting that with you so everything else is just dressing. Whatever we do will be beautiful and memorable."

"Would you consider including the kids in the ceremony?"

"Missy as my bridesmaid?"

"I'll have Kenny as my best man."

"Do they like me enough?"

He brushed her hair back, hooking it behind her ear. "They love you enough. I told you already we're a package deal." Then he kissed her. "Piper, take my name, my hand, my home, my family—my love."

"Gladly." She brushed at her eyes yet again.

He gave her a silly grin. "I promise you this. I'll be faithful, try not to lose my temper too much, and pamper you ridiculously." Then he turned more serious. "I'll take care of you, Piper."

She was touched but she shook her head. "We'll take care of each other and I'm going to start by making sure all of you eat properly from now on."

He laughed. "I hope so. I don't think I can stand another sandwich." Then he kissed her tenderly. "I trust you with them, sweetheart."

Piper pulled back. "But we have a lot to discuss. I mean it. I need to know just how you'll feel when I get involved in parenting. Will we work together or against each other? I don't want your jealousy making it harder for me."

"Have I resented any of your help yet? I think we've made a

pretty good and natural team so far."

She thought back and had to admit that he had a point.

Chad smiled and stroked down her sides then stopped on her hips. "I guess this is a good time to ask whether you want to have kids in the future."

Piper laughed. "I'm getting them already."

"You know what I'm asking. Do you want to add to the family?"

"I don't know. How do you feel?"

"It's not my call."

She frowned. "Of course it is. We should both have a say in it."

He kissed her. "Would you believe me if I said I would be happy either way?"

"Honestly?"

"Sure. I love my kids. I'd probably fall deliriously in love with another but the decision to carry a child isn't mine so I'm not going to pressure you either way."

"I guess I'll have to give it some thought."

"Just keep me posted, let me know if there's anything I can do to help."

"You'll be the first to know."

Chad stiffened beneath her. "We're on the wrong side of the covers."

"Come on." She crawled off of him and when he got up she peeled back the comforter and exposed the sheets. "Thread count?"

"Six hundred?"

"Acceptable." He laughed and she burst out suddenly, "Hey, I have to call my parents and tell them what's going on."

"Can't they wait until tomorrow?"

He gave her an expressive look, framing the obvious with his open hands as he stood there, erect and impatient.

Piper grinned. "Yeah, let them wait."

Chad drew Piper down on the mattress where they proceeded to take a slow and thorough survey of each other's bodies using every means available.

"My god, Piper, you're sexy," he said with a husky catch in his throat.

The look in her eyes was a heady swirl of love and lust. "My thoughts exactly."

He rolled into the center of the bed, taking her with him.

"I love it when you do stuff like that," she said breathlessly.

He laughed. "Like what?"

"Move me, lift me, pick me up. You're so strong and you're not even trying to show off. It's just so incredibly hot."

He grinned. "Oh yeah? Maybe I should do more of that."

"I recommend it."

"Tell me, what do you think of this?"

He drew her up his body then lifting her under the arms, he set her down directly over his face. Chad skimmed his hands lightly down her sides and took hold of her hips, holding her exactly where he wanted her. Then his tongue came out to play.

Piper's pelvis jerked and she gasped. "Okay, yeah, you've got my attention."

She could feel the spread of Chad's smile between her thighs.

"*This* is not the last time," she said sternly.

"Not by a long shot," he said with a chuckle, inhaling the very essence of her. "Honey, I'm home."

Piper's eyes fell closed and she swayed gently, lulled into submission by the loving attentions of the man beneath her. Why had she fought this, fought him—fought herself? Joy was right, he satisfied—oh god, he satisfied—everything she ever wanted from a man.

She'd never been so intimately connected to anyone like this before. She'd feared it, run from it. Now she didn't even understand that early version of herself. She couldn't fathom warning Chad off again. He was her lover, her life, her very future. He was the lottery and every fantasy she ever contemplated all rolled into one. There was always a part of her, there must have been, that recognized immediately that he was going to bring big changes.

He opened her up, loved her, and healed her bruised heart.

Touched and impossibly grateful to him, Piper began to weep. She covered his hand with hers and he wove their fingers together.

He gave her a wet though infinitely tender kiss. "You okay?"

"I'm going to marry you, Chad," she told him, then shuddered as he nuzzled in deeply. With a gasp she let go, feeling all her defensive barriers dissolve in a powerful rush of exquisite bliss.

Then they made love.

Chad watched the woman he loved softly exhale with every slow thrust. Her lashes fluttered sometimes and that made him smile. She had quirks, amusing intoxicating quirks and they had a lifetime to discover all of them together. He couldn't wait.

He leaned down and kissed her tenderly, lingeringly and wove his fingers with hers. He could feel Piper building, swelling tight around him. She rose to him, straining more as she took him deeper. They were both struggling for air but they had time yet and no one was going to interrupt them tonight or force a hasty finish. He smiled, understanding that wasn't always going to be the case.

The kids would be home tomorrow night. He wasn't ashamed of wanting Piper in his bed, as his wife, for their mother, but how would this news go over with them? He'd never introduced a woman into their lives like this before. He supposed they'd find out tomorrow. And they needed to work on Piper's screaming orgasms.

"Why are you smiling?" Piper asked.

"It's nothing," he whispered, giving her another cryptic smile.

He drew his hands free and made a small adjustment to their position. Piper gasped on his next drive.

"Hurt?" he asked with a slight frown.

"Don't you dare stop that."

He smiled and redoubled his efforts and Piper started to hum like a teakettle, her face and chest flushing with heat.

"Oh god, Chad," she cried, her voice trembling.

"What is it sweetheart?" he asked plunging with even more determination once he saw her color flare.

"I can't hold it in," she said panicking.

"Then don't," he said softly. "Let it out, rattle the windows if you have to. I want you to let loose tonight."

She stopped fighting herself and let her fevered eyes defocus. A low wail vibrated up her body, coming from her very depths and escaped through her mouth, making her laugh and weep at the same time. Chad kissed her, swallowing her cry. He could feel it pass through him like a warm red glow traveling down his throat, through his body, finally bursting out of him as white liquid heat right into her again. It was a loving return.

They slept little that night, sharing the double shower around two in the morning before finally falling into a heavy, sated but short sleep with their arms and legs entwined.

29

"I have to take you grocery shopping," Piper said as she reached for the thermal mug of coffee Chad held out to her. "I can't believe you have nothing to eat here besides Fruity O's."

He rolled his eyes and pulled the mug away, holding it high in the air out of her reach. "I told you I don't do breakfast."

"That's going to change," she said trying to take back her mug. "Breakfast is the most important meal of the day. Now give me my coffee. I have to go."

Chad leered at her and leaned down. "For a kiss."

"You had a kiss," she said impatiently. "You had more than a kiss and you know it. You're going to make me late."

"One kiss."

He turned his cheek towards her and she stretched up to deliver a quick peck but he was quicker. His left arm snaked around her waist and pulled her against him, his right redirected her lips. The plastic mug conked Piper in the back of the head but that wasn't the reason her brain went foggy. When Chad finally released her, dazed and distracted, he had to feed her hand through the handle of the mug for her then curl her fingers around it.

"Hold it upright, sweetheart, or you'll spill," he said, quite pleased with himself.

"I'm going to get you for this."

"Promise?" He laughed at the look she shot him as she bolted out the door.

"Drive carefully!" He yelled after her.

Piper gave him a single, silent salute and climbed into the driver's seat. Hers was the only car on the otherwise empty street when she drove away.

Chad went back to bed for two more hours. He was relaxing in the kitchen reading the newspaper with his slipper-covered feet resting on a second kitchen chair when Kenny and Missy burst into the house.

"In the kitchen," he called to them.

They both ran to their father for hello hugs.

"Did you have fun?" he asked.

"Uh huh," Missy nodded. "And we got to make Jell-O."

"No kidding." Chad laughed and gave the side of her head a loving stroke.

"I made sloppy Joes," Kenny told him.

"No, you didn't," Missy countered.

"Yes, I did."

"No, you didn't."

"Well, I helped."

"You hoo!" Alice called from the front door. "I see bags here. Am I supposed to trip on them coming in or what?"

Chad chuckled. "Go bring your stuff to your rooms. Dirty clothes in the hampers please."

"Yes," they grumbled in unison and wandered out, passing their grandmother on her way in.

"How were they?" Chad asked.

"Fine."

She set her purse on the table and took in Chad's appearance, the dark circles under his eyes, the uncombed hair, and dark stubble. "You're not dressed yet?"

Actually he was, but she didn't know that. "I put on a t-shirt."

"You could have put on pants, too. That robe hardly counts."

"I'm covered."

Alice pursed her lips and considered him carefully, her manner softening. "So, it didn't go well then?"

Chad broke into a smile that stretched the boundaries of his face and warmed the entire kitchen.

Alice's eyebrows shot straight up. "What are you saying?"

He shook his head. "Let's wait for the kids."

"In that case, maybe I'd better have a cup of coffee. Something tells me I'm going to need it." She gave him another curious look then went to the cabinet and pulled out a mug.

Chad folded his section of the newspaper and laid it on the rest. "It's probably cold."

"That's what microwaves are for."

Missy was the first one back and she went right to her dad and hopped onto his lap. He wrapped her close and rested his chin on her head. The girl reached up to rub his whiskers.

"Ouch, Daddy, your face is sharp."

"Yeah, I know. Sorry sweetie."

"That's okay. Can I have a juice box?"

"Sure."

Missy hopped down and danced over to the refrigerator.

Kenny wandered in and saw her. "Hey, can I have one too?"

"Yes."

When they were both ready Alice opened the floor. "Your father has something to tell us."

Chad smiled at her. "Thanks, Mom."

Naturally she smiled right back. "Anytime."

With everyone looking at him expectantly, Chad sat up straight and tidied his robe and combed his fingers through his hair before finally confessing, "I asked Piper to marry me last night."

Alice and Missy turned to each other with wide eyes and Alice dropped onto a chair. Kenny just looked astonished. Everyone stared at Chad.

"And?" his mom prompted impatiently.

Chad laughed and to the amazement of everyone he blushed. "She said yes."

His news was met with squeals and shrieks.

"Does this mean that Piper is going to be our mom?" Kenny asked.

"Yes." Chad nodded. "Can you handle it?"

Kenny thought about it for a second. "I guess I don't mind."

Chad got up and whether Kenny was amenable or not, gave him a big manly bear hug. It went over well.

"I had a feeling." Alice shook her finger at Chad as she hugged Missy then dabbed her eyes with a tissue.

"I didn't."

"Have you discussed when?"

"As soon as we can get a license."

"I see." Her amusement was obvious.

"So sue me for wanting to settle things fast," Chad said churlishly.

"I wouldn't dream of it."

Her response made him smile. "Thanks. I thought you'd understand."

"More than you know," she said softly.

That's when it hit him, like a sucker punch. How easily he forgot that they were both widowed in the same year. She really *did* understand his impatience, the emptiness, and the longing to connect with one special person.

"My god, I should have remembered." There was pain and apology in his eyes.

"Honey, it's okay. I didn't expect you to worry about me. You had enough on your plate and you were so young, much too young to be alone. I'm happy for you, for you both." Unshed tears were making her already bright eyes sparkle even more.

He held up a hand and looked at his children. "One more thing. Piper and I want you two in the wedding. Ken, will you be my best man?"

"What do I have to do?"

"Give me Piper's wedding ring when I ask for it."

"I can do that."

"Do I get to hold your ring?" Missy asked.

"Why not?"

"I get flowers, too, right?"

"Yes."

"Yea, I'm going to be in a wedding!" Missy jumped up and down like a rabbit.

The kids raced off to tell their friends the news and Chad was able to get back to the topic that suddenly interested him.

"So, how was your date last week?"

"Fine."

"Just fine?"

Alice blushed and Chad's eyebrows shot up.

"Don't look so shocked," Alice said. "I've been seeing Charles for a while now."

"Charles?" His eyes went impossibly wide now. "Charles Little? Dad's old friend and lawyer?"

"The same and for your information, Charles protected my interests when I sold the banks after your dad died. He looked out for me and made sure I was financially secure."

"That's right, I remember now. How is he?"

"Wonderful. He was always so gracious, so proper and polite, I never expected there was a furnace in his heart, too."

"So you like him." It was a statement, not a question.

She blushed again and looked down, uncomfortable meeting her son's eyes. "Yes, I like him—very much."

"Why didn't you tell me sooner?"

Alice shrugged a shoulder. "I didn't know how you'd take it."

"Mom," Chad reached out and grabbed her hand. "I always wanted you to be happy. I still do."

She patted the back of his hand. "I want that for you, too."

Chad grinned. "Then I think we're wasting our time sticking with this cold coffee. I think it's time to switch to mimosas. What do you say? A little champagne in orange juice seems more fitting. We both have celebrating to do."

"Do you have champagne in the house?"

"No, but I can run for some."

"I'll go. You get upstairs and clean up. You've got a fiancé coming back in a few hours. She shouldn't see you like that."

"She already did, this morning when she left." Chad laughed at the pained expression on his mother's face.

Her hand shot up to stop him. "No need to tell me everything." Alice picked up her purse. "I'll be back in a flash and you'd better be showered and stubble free."

"Promise."

Joy stared at Piper in shock. "That's unbelievable! You and Big Daddy are really tying the knot? That is so fricking amazing I don't know what to think. I'm making your cake."

Piper laughed. "Seriously, you really want to?"

"Yes! Hell yes! I never get to make cakes for people I know, especially not wedding cakes." She dusted the oven door with the towel in her hand and sighed. "Wow, I didn't expect you to be engaged when you came to work today. I just hoped you would have worked things out with Chad. This is so unbelievably incredible!" She laughed again and grabbed hold of Piper, spinning her around excitedly.

"I can't get over how happy I am." Piper thought again of the tender send off Chad gave her that morning. She could get used to that kind of treatment.

"The woman who wouldn't be rushed is rushing to the altar."

"You know why."

"Of course," Joy teased. "You want your Big Daddy."

Piper scrunched up her face. "You know we have to think about the kids, too."

"Admit it, you want him."

Piper's eyes closed and her head fell back. "Every minute of every day. I'm surprised I can function at all."

"Then there's only one thing I need to know."

"What's that?"

"When you'll want your cake."

The wedding took place two weeks later on the deck, the railings festooned with fluttering streamers and simple flower arrangements provided by the store.

Though the ceremony itself was brief, a good thing with two fidgety attendants, the celebration that followed grew into a neighborhood block party as people stopped by to wish the couple well and were asked to stay for cake and punch, this time made by Alice. Joy, cuddling the bridal bouquet like a treasure, was sweet enough to keep Dom out of the kitchen and far away from the punch bowl this time.

Brent and Pam provided the champagne and every glass and cup in the house was eventually put to use by the time the last cork popped.

Pam pulled Piper aside and shook her head. "I can't believe you're not taking a honeymoon."

"I told you, we are, just not until the end of the month. Neither of us can escape work right now. It's the busy season and Chad is knee deep in the Weber construction."

"But that doesn't count. You're taking the kids. What kind of honeymoon is that?"

Piper looked over at lovely Missy in her fairy princess dress and her flower coronet and handsome Kenny, a photographic copy of his father, and smiled. A fast friendship had sprung up between the kids and Piper's father who, after pointing his little penlight into their mouths and inspecting their teeth, had pronounced them perfect. While they bonded over gums and proper brushing her mother was warming up to Alice and Charles Little. Piper's heart softened as she looked at the older gentleman. Sweet Charles hadn't left Alice's side all day. Piper had high hopes for that romance.

Piper turned back and beamed at Pam. She couldn't seem to help herself these days. "Chad and I will have a few nights together right here. Alice is going to take the kids so we can have the house all to ourselves then we'll take a family trip to Disney World later."

Pam rolled her eyes at the ceiling. "I can't imagine."

"We're forming a new family. That's how Chad and I want it."

"You'll have connecting rooms for the kids, right?"

"Of course."

Pam laughed. "At least you have that."

Piper grinned and raised her mug of champagne stamped with the words, Number One Dad on the side. As she swallowed she turned and caught Chad watching her with a thoroughly hungry look in his eyes. She choked on her bubbly, much to Pam's surprise, and received a pat on the back.

"Wrong pipe?" Pam asked with concern.

"I'm fine."

Chad chuckled and excused himself from his group of friends and made his way over to his bride. The way he looked at her set Piper's heart pounding like a Japanese gong.

He spared a quick smile for Pam then tipped down and kissed Piper's neck. "Hi," he breathed into her ear on his way back up.

"Hi," she said back, going weak in the knees and melting against him. He caught her around the waist.

An observant woman, Pam blushed. "I think I'll just go and find my husband. Excuse me."

"Chad, we chased her away. That was rude," Piper said faintly, her rebuke falling flat as her head fell to the side and Chad slid his lips up under her hair.

"I'm sorry, but I can't help myself. You look gorgeous. Think you can spare a few minutes for your husband?"

"What do you have in mind?"

"I know where the laundry room is."

Piper laughed and slapped him lightly on the chest. "Not now."

"When?"

"Soon."

"How soon?"

"We have guests."

"How can we break up the party? I could call the cops."

"Patience is a virtue."

"I make my own virtues."

"Tell me something I don't know."

Chad laughed and wrapped his arm around his wife. "I guess we mingle. I just need to touch you, is that okay?"

"More than okay."

He kissed the top of her head. "Good."

When Chad saw Angela Markland slipping away with his foreman, the potbellied, good-humored Hanson, he wondered if he should warn him but decided against it. Everyone ought to have a clear shot at finding love and Hanson was a big boy. He wished him luck. Who knew, maybe he'd be the man to tame the hot suburban beast.

After the last of their guests finally left, Chad pulled Piper against him and sighed.

"I didn't think I'd ever get you alone, Mrs. Thomas."

He lifted her hand and turned the ring on her finger, admiring the stones for a moment before pressing the band with a tender kiss.

She smiled. "Mrs. Thomas."

He looked at the stairs over her shoulder. "You interested?"

"We've done the stairs. How about a rain check?"

He raised an eyebrow suggestively. "We have a nice laundry room we haven't tried yet."

She considered it, briefly. "You said the appliances were a bit too high."

"For some things, maybe, but I have some interesting ideas." He teased her neck with his teeth and lips.

"Mmm, I'll bet you do." She shimmied against him. "Why don't we start upstairs and work our way down?"

"I'm all yours."

She smiled up at her husband's sparkling eyes and leaned in for a deep and lingering kiss. "Yes, you are."

In the mood for more Crimson Romance? Check out *The Confession* by Erin McCauley at CrimsonRomance.com.

CPSIA information can be obtained at www.ICGtesting.com
Printed in the USA
LVOW070830020313

322389LV00022B/530/P